Ashleigh B.: Blackberries on the Fence

Blackberries on the Fence

by Ashleigh B.

Ashleigh B.: Blackberries on the Fence

EDITED BY JHORDYNN (318) 406-2249

COVER FORMATTED BY

PUBLISHED BY MADE 4 THIS PUBLISHING

ISBN-13 (Paperback): 978-1-7365773-8-7

TABLE OF CONTENTS

TABLE OF CONTENTS

TABLE OF CONTENTS

TABLE OF CONTENTS

<u>DEDICATION</u>

To the ones my heart love most:

Granddaddy, the man who assured I would always feel loved and safe, thank God for the time He allowed you on this Earth. If I had known life would feel so incomplete without you, this tribute would have been written sooner. I dedicate my first book to you. I know you're in heaven smiling hard and rooting me on through this journey. I love you very much, and I will continue to make you proud.

My children: Jayson, Destiney, and Aaron, you have changed my life immensely for the better. I'm blessed God chose me to be your mother. I include you all in every goal, decision, and endeavor. You make life worth living. I'm indebted to you, always. When the world seems too heavy to hold, remember Mommy will forever carry your burdens with you. Continue being your authentic selves. I ask God to allow your life to be as carefree and sweet like the "blackberries on the fence". I love you all with my entire heart.

Ashleigh B.: Blackberries on the Fence

...Sometime in the early 90s

PROLOGUE

Jasmine woke up to her mom and dad standing over her. She had slept so hard that she missed her mama coming through the door from work.

"James say you bit him? I saw your teeth marks on his arm, and he is missing flesh. What has gotten into you? What the hell is wrong with you?! This is your daddy! Not some nigga in the streets! And you are a lady! What is wrong with you?!" her mom, Shelia, asked her.

"Did James ever tell you why I did? Because I was tired of him coming into my room every night sticking his pissy dick in me!"

Shelia slapped her.

"You slap *me* over what *your* husband did?!"

"You are lying! You are just so full of antics and drama! Jasmine, I swear you should write books when you grow up so you can direct this imagination of yours somewhere! But lies belong in books, not in this house! You will pay for what you did to your daddy!"

Jasmine's body was full of bruises. Those bruises were the proof of what James had been doing to her. Some were old. Some were new. If she showed Shelia those bruises, Shelia would have no choice but to believe Jasmine because Shelia had never gotten a call that Jasmine had been in a fight at school. Robert, Michelle, nor Denise ever told Shelia that Jasmine had been fighting them. A neighbor never told Shelia that Jasmine was in the streets fighting. Shelia would have no choice but to swallow and accept that the bruises on Jasmine's body happened in *her* house by *her* husband!

But Jasmine decided against showing her mom her bruises. She knew that Shelia would find a reason to continue to be in denial and protect James. That would hurt Jasmine even more—to know that her mom one hundred percent knew and did nothing. Or maybe Shelia would actually do something about it with the proof staring her dead in her face. But there was no way for Jasmine to know that for sure. She'd rather assume that Shelia would do nothing than to know for a fact that she would do nothing. So Jasmine sat there and accepted the accusation that she was the predator.

Shelia stood there, lips quivering, eyes closed. Somehow, Shelia convinced herself that closing her eyes would make this situation not exist. Deep down, she'd known for years what was happening. But she figured if she prayed about it, it would go away. What else was she supposed to do? Press charges against her own husband? Divorce the father of her kids?

Let's be real. Both scenarios would be too embarrassing. She prided herself in being married before she had children. Remaining married to her children's father was the highlight of her life. All of her biological children having the same dad was always the topic of conversation at work. And he provided well. He was a manager at a plant. Their income together made their lifestyle possible.

If she left him, that would be over fifty percent of the income leaving the house. She would have to move and downgrade. And oh, my God. What would she drive? She would have to trade in her SUV for a *car*. What would she tell her friends and coworkers and church members?

No. All of that would be too messy. Too, too messy. Jasmine was causing too much discord and tension in the house. She had to go.

Chapter 1

"Come here, Blackberry!" Wallace lovingly called out to his granddaughter Jasmine. "Let's pick some blackberries off the fence."

Wallace didn't necessarily do anything with the blackberries. He didn't bake pies with them, he didn't use them to color or stain anything. He rarely ate them. It was just his favorite pastime with Jasmine. She was so quiet and always to herself. But he noticed that when they picked blackberries off the fence together, she would open up and talk more than usual. No, it didn't make her a "Chatty Cathy", but he got more than the usual two words out of her.

Jasmine had a love-hate relationship with picking the blackberries off the fence. Her abusive dad also called her Blackberry, so picking blackberries was a trigger for her. It was a reminder of all that her dad put her through. Picking blackberries made her relive moments she prayed so hard to forget.

Adding to the trigger, her hands would be so sore from fighting off her dad, and her wrists would be extremely sore and bruised from her dad holding her down. Picking blackberries only added to the pain and discomfort. She always wore gloves when it was time to pick the blackberries so that Wallace wouldn't see the evidence of a "ruined girl", as the

1

residents of Baton Rouge called the girls who had suffered any kind of sexual assault.

Baton Rouge, Louisiana, being the south, had a lot of slave mentality plaguing the streets and offensive lingo. A girl who had been raped was seen as ruined, damaged goods, wasted, defected, whorish, and fast. As if she "chose" to be held down, drugged, sex trafficked, etcetera, whatever the case may be. Point was, she was now open and no more good. Didn't matter why. A man or men had been inside her. She served no purpose anymore. She wasn't pure anymore. She wasn't whole anymore. She was a disservice and a dishonor to her husband.

If she didn't want to be any of that, she shouldn't have been raped. Now that she'd been raped, that good girl ship has sailed. She better not fix her mind to even want a good man. She didn't deserve a good man because she was now open. She had to accept whatever man came along. That was the price to pay for being raped.

To some extent, they knew that the girl was a victim, but people in the south believed in praying and saying nothing. Praying and doing nothing. Praying and talking about folks. Praying and judging. But praying and *changing,* well, that was a different story.

No matter how progressive Black people had become, no matter how much times had changed, the south was a constant reminder that slavery was only a few generations ago. No, not *all* people in the south were this way. There were plenty of Black congressmen and Black civilians fighting for change. There were plenty of White people fighting alongside Black people for a difference. But collectively, generally, as a whole, the south was the south.

Unbeknownst to Wallace, Jasmine hated being called Blackberry. Her dad James called her that one day when she was an infant, and it stuck with Wallace. Wallace called her that lovingly because he knew that she would need a constant reminder that Black is beautiful. She was very dark skinned, and it would be easy for her to believe the lies that she was "too dark", "too shiny", "too greasy". He wanted to get ahead of the game. He wanted his voice to ring in her ears every time she heard that her skin made her ugly because he knew that she would definitely hear it.

That part of his plan worked. She was fifteen and had heard how ugly she was fifteen million times. But her granddad had been calling her Blackberry, Black, and Chocolate Babydoll ever since she was a baby. Those insults that her classmates and others threw at her did nothing to her.

He loved calling her Blackberry because "the darker the berry, the sweeter the juice". He meant that as in "the darker you are, the more valuable you are". No one wants bitter fruit. But she was "bitter fruit" in her own way. It fit anyway because

Jasmine felt that blackberries were the most bitter fruit God ever created, despite how black they were.

Even though Wallace meant it innocently, for a girl who had been getting raped by her dad since she was nine years young, that sounded sexual and made her cringe. "The sweeter the juice" made her feel like she was on an auctioning block for men to bid on her. Especially because whenever her dad would say "the sweeter the juice", she knew exactly what he meant and how he meant it.

"What's going on in your world, Blackberry?" Paw Paw Wallace asked her, as they walked along the quarter-mile fence picking blackberries.

"I hate geometry."

"Well, I shole can't help you there. Only thing I knew about geometry was that your grandma had a shape that was just right for me!"

Jasmine shook her head and laughed. "I don't want to hear that." She joked. "Disgusting!"

"Disgusting? How you think we got your mama and aunty here? How you think she got you here? Shapes fitting into shapes!"

"Paw Paw, that is not geometry. That is anatomy and physiology. And I'm doing just fine in that class."

"You sure you don't need my help with that subject? Shit. You'll be Valedictorian then."

"I'm so sure." Jasmine laughed.

"Well, I'm so sure that you need to take these gloves off. You taking the joy out of picking berries, which ya saditty ass."

"I don't want to get stuck by the thorns."

" 'I don't want to get stuck by the thorns,' " he mocked her.

"I have hands to protect. I'm going to be a surgeon one day."

"And when you do, I will buy you your first box of gloves."

They smiled at each other and continued to pick the blackberries off the fence. That was the only conversation he got out of her that day, and he was so grateful to God for that. She said more than she had in a while.

Chapter 2

"*Sometimes, my vision is a little hazy. I can't tell who I should trust or just who I let trust me… What about your friends? Will they stand their ground? Will they let you down*?…," Jasmine sang, as she cleaned up around the house.

"I usually don't like the music that you listen to, but I like this song. Who sings that?" Jasmine's mom Shelia asked her.

"TLC."

"Tender, Love, and Care?"

"T-Boz, Left Eye, and Chilli," Jasmine dryly answered her.

"What that hell is a Bozo, Low Eye, and Chili Beans?"

"That's their names."

"They made a good song, but Good Lord. Who is their manager? Who is their advocate? They'll never go far with those names. This will be their first, only, and last hit, I'm sure. Mark my words."

Jasmine wasn't going to go into details about how TLC already had multiple hits, nor how they were a Black girl group killing the game. The things Shelia did know, she did nothing about, so why tell her things she knew nothing about? There were more pressing matters at hand.

"You been cleaning all day. Why are you so slow?"

"My hands hurt, Mama. I'm doing the best I can."

"Your hands wouldn't hurt if you weren't such a tomboy. Out there playing basketball got your hands hurting like that." Shelia looked at Jasmine for a reaction—to see if she'd nonverbally agree or disagree with her accusation of why her hands and wrists hurt. Jasmine was nonchalant and flat; she was unreadable.

"I'm heading to work." Shelia changed the subject. "Make sure your sisters and brother stay in line. Don't call me at work with no foolishness. I'll see you tomorrow if God says the same."

Shelia worked overnight from six thirty pm to seven am as a dispatcher. She had four children and a lifestyle that she desired and had to maintain. Barely over minimum wage dispatcher jobs didn't cut it, so she worked seven days a week most weeks between three overnight dispatcher jobs.

Jasmine used to hate to see the door close behind her mom because that signified that the abuse from her dad was about to begin. But her dad had gotten so bold that he stopped waiting for his wife to leave; as long as Shelia was asleep, he did what he did.

Crash! Jasmine ran to the kitchen to see what caused the noise. Her twelve-year-old brother Robert was sitting at the kitchen table eating a snack.

"How did glass get on the floor, Robert?" Jasmine asked him.

"I dropped a glass," he answered, rolling his eyes.

"Then clean it up before somebody steps on it and gets hurt."

"Nobody in the house is blind. If they step on it, they're stupid and deserve to be bleeding."

"Clean up your mess, Robert! Now!"

"You clean it up! You're the one worried about it."

"I'm not cleaning up your mess!"

"Jasmine, clean up this glass off the floor. You're cleaning up already anyway. Don't be so dramatic about it," her dad James told her, as he walked into the kitchen. "And watch your tone with him. He's just a kid."

"A kid who needs to be taught something," she mumbled underneath her breath.

She got the broom and began sweeping.

"Would've been a shame if your baby sisters walked in and stepped on this glass and got caught. All that time you spent fussing, you could have been cleaning," James said. "You ready for your football game tomorrow night, Son?" James asked Robert.

"Yep," Robert answered.

If Jasmine or her ten-year-old sister Michelle or five-year-old sister Denise would answer an adult "Yep", their heads would get knocked off their shoulders. It better be "Yes, Ma'am or No, Ma'am", "Yes, Sir or No, Sir". But Robert got away with any and everything. He was their dad's favorite, and that was a secret to no one.

"You been practicing throwing that ball like I taught you?"

"Uh huh. Sure have. Every day."

"And what about the tips I gave you to run faster?"

"Fa sho'. I'm on it, Pops."

"You sure?"

"James, I said I got it."

Robert was the only person who got away with calling their dad by his name. Not even James's wife could call him by his name.

"And you standing in the shade whenever you can, right? Don't mess up that light skin of yours. That's how you get all the hoes."

"I put on sunscreen and stand in the shade. Ain't nothing finna mess up my pretty skin. All them hoes on me."

"Good. I know you wanted to play basketball, but I told you football was better. It's more masculine, makes you stronger, and the bitches love it." James directed his conversation to Jasmine. "Jasmine, get Denise and Michelle to help you clean up. You been taking all day. Time to wrap this up."

"I enjoy cleaning. I'm fine. They don't need to help me."

"I know you ain't talking back, you burnt piece of coal!" James fired off at Jasmine.

"Oh, no. I know I'm not Robert. I could never do that."

She walked out of the kitchen and began dusting the living room.

Michelle went to the living room with a vacuum and whispered into Jasmine's ear, "They make diamonds out of coal."

Jasmine smirked at that comment. Michelle was absolutely right.

"Pressured coal makes diamonds," Jasmine said to herself.

Michelle had no idea how much her big sister needed to hear that. Jasmine whispered that to herself over and over that night as her dad sexually assaulted her. *"One day, I'mma be a diamond. I won't always be ruined."*

Chapter 3

"Jasmine, you won't be going out there to pick no blackberries today. You gonna stay in here and help prepare the food and set the table like a lady," Grandma Darlene said, as she kissed Jasmine on her cheek.

Jasmine was so relieved. She hated picking them damn blackberries! The assault was fresh from less than twelve hours ago. She was too sore to do work like that. She could easily find less strenuous work in the kitchen. As long as she looked busy, Grandma Darlene wouldn't trip.

She loved her granny. She and her siblings affectionately called her Grams. But who didn't love Grams? She was the textbook grandma: always had a hot meal on the stove, fed the neighborhood, gave everyone a ride to church, remembered everyone's birthdays, gave the mailman a Christmas present, kept fresh baked cookies in a tin. The list goes on and on. Jasmine hated sharing her with everybody. She wished that Grams would save a little bit of herself just for Jasmine.

"Coulda been me outdoors, with no food, and no clothes. Or just alone without a friend. Or just another number with a tragic end...," Darlene sang as she prepared the food.

"What's on the menu today, Grams?" Michelle asked her.

11

"Nothing major today. Grams getting old. Just some black-eyed peas, buttermilk cornbread, fried chicken, cabbage, sweet potatoes, mashed potatoes, shrimp and grits, and bone-in steak. I only had time to bake a buttermilk pie and Seven Up poundcake. Y'all not finna have me slaving like that. Take it or leave it."

"Where's the smothered turkey necks? I'mma leave it."

"You are one ungrateful heathen." Darlene and Michelle laughed together. "That'll be the day your greedy self pass up some food. You'll eat a steering wheel if I put some salt on it."

"Grams! You are right." Michelle laughed. "Jasmine, hand me that tin can, please. I want a cookie."

"Grams, can you give this to Michelle, please?" Jasmine asked, as she passed Grams the tin can.

Grams hesitantly took the can from her. *Have I not been paying attention? Has my attention been other places to where I didn't notice this in my own granddaughter? What is all this on her wrists?* Grams thought to herself. She gave the tin can to Michelle and walked out of the room.

"You got lucky today. Paw Paw usually has you out there picking them blackberries. I don't know why you hate it. I love it. I wish he would ask me to go," Michelle told Jasmine.

"I wish you could go in my place."

Jasmine continued to put the dishes in the cabinet. She decided that after all the dishes were put up, she'd take out all the seasonings and groceries that Grams needed to do her cooking. This kitchen work still hurt her hands, but not as bad as picking them damn berries.

"Black! Come help me pick these berries off the fence!" Paw Paw called out to Jasmine.

Grams walked into the kitchen.

"Grams! Tell him that you have me in here doing kitchen work," Jasmine whined.

"Do what Paw Paw says," Grams replied.

Jasmine couldn't believe it. Grams always had her back, always came to her rescue. What did she mean by "Do what Paw Paw says"? *Save me!* But one thing Grams didn't do was go against her husband. And Jasmine found out that day that Grams didn't even go against her husband for her.

Jasmine stomped away and went to the drawer to put on her gloves. But the gloves weren't there! She always kept them there. As a matter of fact, she kept two to three pairs of gloves in there. She had been keeping them there for the last three years. She started fighting her dad back when she was twelve; that's when the bruises began.

"Michelle," Jasmine whispered, "where are my gloves?"

"I don't know. But if you just pick the berries the way Paw Paw showed us, you wouldn't need them anyway."

"But. But. There are none in this drawer. How are there *none*?"

"I. Don't. Know. Just pick the berries like Paw Paw showed us."

"You got molasses in your ass? Come on, Gal!" Paw Paw called out to Jasmine from the living room.

"I just don't want Paw Paw to see all these bruises on my wrists," Jasmine whispered to Michelle.

"Why you tripping over nothing? You got them from an allergic reaction to something, and it never went away. Why you care if he sees that?"

"You right. Nothing. It's me. I'm just tripping."

Jasmine and Paw Paw picked blackberries off the fence for three minutes before Paw Paw started up a conversation.

"How's geometry going?"

"I still hate it. I have a B in the class."

"Damn. You have a B in something you hate. What you make in the classes you love? Triple As?"

"You are so corny, Paw Paw."

"I hate corn. Tell me I'm so Peas-y. Easy peasy as a matter of fact." Wallace laughed at his own joke until tears flowed down his face. "I missed my calling, Chocolate Doll, I tell you that. I would put Richard Pryor and Eddie Murphy out of commission."

"Stick to driving trucks, Paw Paw." Jasmine laughed.

They continued walking and picking blackberries off the fence.

"What happened to your wrists?" he asked her.

"I had an allergic reaction to something. I don't know what it was. But I broke out."

"Okay. I heard that a dead body makes real good fertilizer. They say it makes whatever you're growing grow ten times faster."

"Um. That's kind of disgusting."

"You know what fertilizer is? It's shit. All that watermelon you eat grew from shit. What's the difference? Ain't like you're eating the dead body just like ain't like you eating the shit."

"I don't know, Paw Paw. We be eating it some kind of way. I don't know. But anyway, what you gone do? Go down to the cemetery, dig up somebody, plant 'em in your back yard, and speed up the time it takes to grow your blackberries?"

"Not a bad idea, Black. You know it can take up to two years for these blackberries to grow? It don't seem like it because the seeds have already been planted, and I keep planting seeds, so there's always blackberries out here. But I want to plant another tree and a bush and sell some blackberries.

"You know I always catch folks trynna steal 'em off my fence. I would make a killing if I had a heap more. I just hate the thought of waiting two years. I know. Two years from now, I'mma wish I woulda did it. But if I could get 'em to grow in a month or two, whew! I would have motivation to plant that tree and bush and sell me some blackberries."

"Enjoy yourself, Paw Paw. Leave me out of that."

"Well, let's go back in the house. These berries ain't ready. Guess we done picked 'em all."

Chapter 4

"The blacker the berry, the sweeter the juice," James said, as the rattle from his belt buckle could be heard. "The darker the flesh, the *deeper* the roots." His pants hit the ground. "Now, I would never do this to Michelle or Denise. I don't want to mess up their pretty yellow skin. But you, you can take it. It don't make you no never mind. Can't nothing be done to yo' black ass to make you worse."

James had been assaulting Jasmine from a young age. She had almost been groomed into thinking this was supposed to happen. She had sort of learned to "lay there and take it". She didn't fight back as much. Never in all those years had she made a sound because she didn't want to wake anyone in the house up.

But tonight was different. She had mentally grown up a little bit. She knew that this wasn't the way life was supposed to go. This was not okay. When she woke up that morning, she made a vow that last time was the last time.

He walked over to Jasmine and began to climb on top of her. Jasmine bit his arm so hard that blood squirted out and his skin was in her teeth. The white meat on his arm was exposed.

"You fucking tar bitch!"

"I'll be that today! Come on, Motherfucker!" she yelled at him.

He choked her and demanded that she never do that again.

The commotion woke Michelle up. Her room was across from Jasmine's room. Michelle always slept with her door cracked. Night after night, she would see her dad leaving Jasmine's room. She never told anyone what she saw or what she thought she saw. He was James. He did no wrong. You shut up when it came down to him.

This night, her door was more cracked than usual, and she saw more than she usually saw. She was stunned when she saw her dad standing there with his penis out. She was young and didn't have full understanding, but she knew that was not a scene that should have existed.

"Close your door, or you'll be next!" James yelled at Michelle, once he saw her looking.

Michelle ran and closed her door. She never told anyone what she saw or what she thought she saw. James put his clothes on and told Jasmine, "Wait 'til I tell your mama in the morning when she comes home."

Jasmine went to the couch and went to sleep, waiting on her mom to get home. She would put everything on the table once her mom made it home. She decided she would tell her mama before James told her mama. She wanted to get to her mama first.

She suspected that her mom knew that he was raping her, but she was going to make sure she knew. Jasmine was going to leave no room for questions or suspicions. She was going to make it crystal clear.

That was the most peaceful sleep she'd had in six years. She knew that he wouldn't bother her ever again. She even had dreams that night. It had been years since she slept good enough to dream.

"Jasmine! Jasmine! Get up right now! What is going on?"

Jasmine woke up to her mom and dad standing over her. She had slept so hard that she missed her mama coming through the door from work.

"James say you bit him? I saw your teeth marks on his arm, and he is missing flesh. What has gotten into you? What the hell is wrong with you?! This is your daddy! Not some nigga in the streets! And you are a lady! What is wrong with you?!"

"Did James ever tell you why I did? Because I was tired of him coming into my room every night sticking his pissy dick in me!"

Shelia slapped her.

"You slap *me* over what *your* husband did?!"

"You are lying! You are just so full of antics and drama! Jasmine, I swear you should write books when you grow up so you can direct this imagination of yours somewhere! But lies belong in books, not in this house! You will pay for what you did to your daddy!"

Jasmine's body was full of bruises. Those bruises were the proof of what James had been doing to her. Some were old. Some were new. If she showed Shelia those bruises, Shelia would have no choice but to believe Jasmine because Shelia had never gotten a call that Jasmine had been in a fight at school. Robert, Michelle, nor Denise ever told Shelia that Jasmine had been fighting them. A neighbor never told Shelia that Jasmine was in the streets fighting. Shelia would have no choice but to swallow and accept that the bruises on Jasmine's body happened in *her* house by *her* husband!

But Jasmine decided against showing her mom her bruises. She knew that Shelia would find a reason to continue to be in denial and protect James. That would hurt Jasmine even more—to know that her mom one hundred percent knew and did nothing. Or maybe Shelia would actually do something about it with the proof staring her dead in her face. But there was no way for Jasmine to know that for sure. She'd rather assume that Shelia would do nothing than to know for a fact that she would do nothing. So Jasmine sat there and accepted the accusation that she was the predator.

Shelia stood there, lips quivering, eyes closed. Somehow, Shelia convinced herself that closing her eyes would make this situation not exist. Deep down, she'd known for years what was happening. But she figured if she prayed about it, it would go away. What else was she supposed to do? Press charges against her own husband? Divorce the father of her kids?

Let's be real. Both scenarios would be too embarrassing. She prided herself in being married before she had children. Remaining married to her children's father was the highlight of her life. All of her biological children having the same dad was always the topic of conversation at work. And he provided well. He was a manager at a plant. Their income together made their lifestyle possible.

If she left him, that would be over fifty percent of the income leaving the house. She would have to move and downgrade. And oh, my God. What would she drive? She would have to trade in her SUV for a *car*. What would she tell her friends and coworkers and church members?

No. All of that would be too messy. Too, too messy. Jasmine was causing too much discord and tension in the house. She had to go.

"You're going to go live with Rosalyn and Daniel. Pack your stuff. Now!" Shelia told Jasmine.

"And where is Daddy going?" Jasmine asked her.

"Hurry up, Jasmine," Shelia told her.

"Where is Daddy going to move to?"

"You are wasting time, Jasmine."

"Wow. You know that I was telling the truth. But you are still going to choose a sick child rapist over your child. You have to live with your decision, not me."

Jasmine went to her room, packed her things, and left anything she didn't need behind.

"Let's go, Jasmine," Shelia told her. "Rosalyn and Daniel are waiting on you."

"I'll have Paw Paw to take me."

"No, the fuck you won't!" Shelia roared at her. "Daddy is not to know anything that goes on in this house. Do you understand me?"

Jasmine said nothing.

"Do you understand me?!"

"Sure."

"Jasmine, I swear to God that if you tell Daddy or anybody about this, you will never be seen again. Give me time to pray about this!"

"Okay."

"Don't play with me, Little Girl."

"I said okay."

"Okay."

"And what do I tell Paw Paw when he asks why I'm living with your sister and her husband? Your sister who hates you? It doesn't even make sense why you would send me to live with someone you don't even get along with."

"I will handle Daddy. I've known him twenty years longer than you. Daddy will blow all of this out of proportion. And you know he doesn't love Jesus the way we do. He wouldn't understand, and he damn sure wouldn't give grace. Daddy shoots first and asks questions later. But later be too late. Just—I will handle this."

Jasmine was never going to tell Wallace. She just wanted to see Shelia squirm. Jasmine knew the truth would kill Wallace. She was his baby, and he couldn't handle anything happening to her. He would blame himself, and Jasmine didn't want to see that. She didn't want to see her granddad hurting.

And what if Wallace tried to hurt James, but James overpowered him and killed Wallace? Jasmine would never be able to live with herself. She'd take her own life if that happened. She had to protect Paw Paw. She would take this to her grave.

Chapter 5

Even though Rosalyn was her favorite aunt, Jasmine wasn't too familiar with her Aunt Rosalyn and Uncle Daniel. Rosalyn and Shelia were sisters who didn't set horses. Jasmine overheard grown folks saying that Rosalyn was jealous of Shelia because Shelia could have children, and Rosalyn couldn't. Jasmine had also overheard that Rosalyn hated Jasmine because she was the first representation of Shelia being able to do something that she couldn't do: have a baby.

But Jasmine never felt hate coming from her. Rosalyn was always loving and caring towards Jasmine whenever they crossed paths. Jasmine could always count on a gift from Rosalyn, whether it be her birthday, Christmas, graduation, or Honor Roll. She even still got Easter baskets from Rosalyn, and she was now sixteen years old.

No, Jasmine couldn't tell you Rosalyn's favorite color, favorite genre of books and movies, or even where she worked. But she did know that whenever Aunt Rosalyn was around, she felt loved, seen, and cared about. So, whatever the adults were talking about when they said that Rosalyn hated Jasmine, she had no idea. There was zero proof of Rosalyn's hate towards Jasmine.

Some people also said Rosalyn was jealous of Shelia because James made a decent amount of money, and her husband, Daniel, didn't. They were damn near poor, and Shelia and James weren't. Yes, Shelia worked seven days a week between multiple jobs, but that got Shelia and James where they wanted to be. Rosalyn was a school administrator, and Daniel was a cashier at a fast-food restaurant. Rosalyn had to foot most of the bills and take care of Daniel in a sense. Being a school administrator didn't leave room for her to get a second job, let alone a third like Shelia. Daniel worked extra shifts, but the extra still was subpar.

The little that Jasmine knew about Rosalyn and Daniel, she loved. They were funny, down to earth, and easy to talk to. She hated that they didn't have kids, though. She would have loved to have cousins to grow up with, talk to, play with. She had aunts and uncles and cousins on her daddy side, but that's a whole different story.

"This is temporary. Just until we sort some things out in our home," Shelia told Rosalyn.

"Jasmine is our niece. It's no problem. That is what family is for."

"Go on in there, Jasmine." Shelia pulled Jasmine close to her and through grit teeth said, "And don't you say shit about shit."

Jasmine walked into the house, spoke, and sat on the couch. Shelia left.

"I know you don't know us well, but that's soon going to change. Tell us about you, and we'll tell you about us," Uncle Daniel said to Jasmine.

Jasmine shrugged her shoulders and shook her head.

"Okay. When you're ready." Daniel sat down beside Jasmine, and she immediately scooted away from him. "I apologize. I didn't mean to cross a boundary."

"That's okay," Jasmine said, barely above a whisper.

Jasmine barely knew her Aunt Rosalyn; she damn sure didn't know her Uncle Daniel. She could pick him out in a line up, but that was about it. He worked a lot. And Jasmine had heard the grown folks say that Paw Paw Wallace didn't like Daniel because Daniel started dating Rosalyn when she was a little girl. Jasmine didn't know their ages, so she didn't know whether that was true or not. But they looked the same age to Jasmine, so in her mind, the most damage that was done was Aunt Rosalyn was sixteen, and Uncle Daniel was eighteen. Yes, illegal. But not sickening illegal. It was understandable illegal.

Another reason she heard that Paw Paw Wallace didn't like Daniel was because Daniel just didn't have shit to offer Rosalyn. Now that sounded like truth to Jasmine. Daniel didn't have shit. He didn't seem to be motivated or determined to have shit, either from Jasmine's point of view. He seemed content with being dusty. But Jasmine also had to keep in mind that she didn't know him, so her observations could be plain wrong.

"I'll tell you about me. I was raised by my mama's parents. My mom died during childbirth with me, like so many other Black women did during that time. My dad drank himself to death when I was two. I know my dad's parents real good. They always been around and there for me. But nothing like Mama's mama and daddy."

Jasmine surely could agree with that.

"I got two sisters older than me that my grandparents raised with me. All my grandparents still alive. Both my sisters dykin', so ain't no kids coming from them.

"I'm allergic to damn peanut butter. My favorite food is them got damn Natchitoches meat pies. My favorite drink is red Kool-Aid. I ain't no dessert eater. My favorite color is red. And I love my Sega Genesis. As long as you don't touch that, we gone be friends."

Jasmine chuckled and nodded her head.

"And you know me. I ain't gotta do no introduction," Rosalyn said.

But Jasmine didn't know her. At this point, she knew more about Daniel than she did her own mama's sister. She wanted to know more about Rosalyn, but Rosalyn seemed to think that Jasmine knew her already.

"What you want to eat today? Your choice," Rosalyn said.

Jasmine had no appetite. She knew her aunt and uncle meant well. She just wanted to sleep. And when she woke up, she wanted to wake up to a different life. This one wasn't it.

27

"I know you don't talk much, but you gotta at least let us know if you're allergic to something. We ain't trynna make no ER visits," Daniel said.

"Seafood," Jasmine answered.

"God must hate you." Daniel joked. "Living in South Louisiana and can't eat seafood. Damn!"

"You allergic to all seafood? Or just shelled?" Rosalyn asked her, shocked.

"All," Jasmine answered.

"Whew," Daniel whistled. "Can you be around it? Smell it? Like, if a jar of peanut butter is open, I get to itching."

"Yes, I can be around seafood," Jasmine answered. "As long as I don't touch it or swallow it."

"Okay. Good. Because we eat a lot of seafood in this house. We'll just make sure we wash our hands real good," Daniel said.

"Thank you."

"You're welcome. Make yourself at home. If you think of anything you want to do or eat, let us know," Rosalyn said.

"Yes, Ma'am."

Jasmine laid on the couch for the rest of the day reading urban lit. The only appetite she had was for turning the pages. She got up only when she had to pee.

She wasn't comfortable enough to "make herself at home". She wasn't even comfortable enough to drink a glass of water. She went to sleep on an empty stomach and woke up with a dry mouth. Even though they were very friendly, warm, and welcoming, her aunt and uncle were strangers to her. She didn't feel right being there. And on top of that, she would now have to walk to school. Her aunt and uncle lived too close to her school for a bus to pick her up. She flat out hated being there. She couldn't wait for the weekend so that she could spend time with her grandparents.

Chapter 6

Aunt Rosalyn and Uncle Daniel worked a lot, so Jasmine had to fend for herself a lot of the time. Good thing was they lived in an area where a lot of things were accessible by foot, so Jasmine could walk almost anywhere she wanted to go. She could even walk to her parents' house if she wanted to, but she never wanted to.

She often walked to the library. She was a nerd, and everyone knew it. She always had her head in a book. For her thirteenth birthday, she begged her grandparents for the entire Britannica encyclopedia collection. When they got it for her, she didn't leave her room for days. Her head was buried in the volumes.

Every time she walked to the library, there would be a man standing outside his car in front of a house. He usually would just be smoking, shooting the shit with other dudes in the hood, or just sitting in his car, jamming to his radio. He wouldn't be causing no trouble, but you could look at him and tell that he was a troublemaker. And that excited Jasmine for all the wrong reasons.

This day when she walked by him, he had a Boombox on his shoulder, blasting music, and rapping, "*I love it when you call me Big Poppa. Throw your hands in the air if you's a true player. I love it when you call me Big Poppa. To the honeys gettin' money, playin' niggas like dummies. I love it when you call me Big Poppa. You got a gun up in your waist, please don't shoot up the place. Why? 'Cause I see some ladies tonight that should be havin' my baby. Baby.*" He pointed at Jasmine. "You! You should be havin' my baby. What's up, Li'l Mama?"

Good Lord, he was fine. He looked intoxicatingly evil. He had sexy bedroom eyes, cuts in his eyebrows that he purposely did. He had a low haircut with a part on the side and waves in his hair. He had on a backwards cap and heavily starched jeans. He knew how fine he was. And my God, his perfect smile with the white teeth that shined like diamonds. It was as if Jesus Himself handcrafted this man, looked at him, said, "Naw, I can do better," did better, and shocked his daggone self.

He wasn't the typical good-looking man. He was dark skinned. The only men who could pull off being dark skinned and fine were Wesley Snipes and Denzel Washington. But add this man to the list. He wouldn't even look good no other shade, except for tar black.

Jasmine kept walking, blushing on the inside. She knew he was no good… but damn, he was fine. And he looked like he smelled so damn good.

"You hear me talking to you! Say, Li'l Mama! Come here!"

"I can't hear you over Biggie Smalls!" Jasmine yelled back.

"Oh, you got jokes. Okay." He turned the music off. "Can you hear me now?"

"A little bit."

"Then come here. You heard that."

Jasmine walked across the street and stopped at his car.

"What's your name, Li'l Mama?"

"Jasmine."

"Yeah, you Jazzy alright." He smirked.

"What's your name?" she asked him.

"E."

"E?"

"E."

"So, if I look on your birth certificate, it'll say E?"

"Naw. It'll say Edward. That old ass lame shit. My mama named me after my granddad."

"It's a distinguished name."

"I ain't no distinguished nigga."

"Maybe you should try it."

"Not in my blood, Shawty."

"Well, I'm on my way to the library. I'll see you later, *Edward*."

"I'll drive you. Get in."

She knew better than to get in the cars with strangers and to ride in cars with boys… but he smelled so good. He smelled better than she thought he would smell.

"Girl, get in the car. Ain't nobody finna do nothing to you."

She hopped in the car faster than she should have.

"You in a rush to get to that library? Or can we ride around a li'l bit?"

"The library can wait."

"I bet it can." He put a cassette tape in the car stereo system. "Listen to these lyrics."

The tape played, "*Life. I wonder. Will it take me under. I don't know. Imagine smoking weed in the streets without cops harassin'. Imagine going to court with no trial. Lifestyle, cruising blue Bahama waters. No welfare supporters. More conscious of the way we raise our daughters… Your people holding dough, no parole, no rubbers. Go in raw. Imagine law with no undercovers. Just some thoughts for the mind. I take a glimpse into time. Watch the blimp read, 'The world is mine'…*"

Jasmine rapped along with the tape, "*So many years of depression make me vision the better livin' type of place to raise kids in. Open they eyes to the lies history's told foul. But I'm as wise as the old owl, plus the gold child… If I ruled the world. Imagine that. I'd free all my sons. I love 'em, love 'em, Baby. Black diamonds and pearls. Could it be? If you could be mine, we'd both shine. If I ruled the world. Still livin' for today in these last days and times.*"

E stared at Jasmine in disbelief. "Wow. You know this song?"

"Shit, it's my anthem." She continued to rap her favorite song in the whole wide world. " *'Cause you could have all the chips, be poor or rich. Still nobody want a nigga havin' shit. If I ruled the world and everything in it, sky's the limit… Strictly living longevity to the destiny I thought I'd never see, but reality struck. Better find out before your time's out…"*

"I see your geeky ass always walking to and from the library. You always got some book in your hand. Always got a backpack on your back. And you spittin' Nas word for word?"

"I love Nas. And Lauryn Hill. This song gonna be a classic. When it's twenty years from now, and people are still rapping this song, remember I said it would happen."

"What was your favorite song before this?" E asked Jasmine.

" 'Superstar.' " Jasmine laughed. She knew that was just proving his point that she was geeky.

"Long ago, and oh, so far away. I fell in love with you before the second show and your guitar. And you sound so sweet and clear. But you're not really hear. It's just the radio," E sang, shocking Jasmine.

They sang together, *"Don't you remember you told me you love me, Baby? You said you'll be coming back this way again. Baby, Baby, Baby, Baby, oh, Baby. Yeah. I love you. I really do.."*

"Oh, wow! Now, what your thuggin' ass know about Luther Vandross?"

"I know that Fat Luther is better than Skinny Luther. Skinny Luther ain't hitting them notes like

Fat Luther be! Them neck rolls be helpin' that nigga out!"

"Shut up!" Jasmine laughed.

"Naw. The question is what *you* know about that song? You had to be a baby when that song came out."

"My granddaddy don't play nothing but Luther. Nobody else these days can sing, if you ask him. Real music died with his generation, let him tell it."

"Well, Gramps ain't wrong."

"What's your favorite song?" she asked him.

"Nah. You already testing my gangsta with Luther. We ain't finna go there."

"Tell me," she whined, while laughing.

E looked at her. He couldn't resist those doll-like eyes. " 'Choosey Lover' by The Isley Brothers."

"*I'm so glad you chose me, Baby. Baby. And I'll make you so happy...*," Jasmine sang.

"You just a radio, ain't cha? What song don't you know?!"

"Music is my man," Jasmine answered.

"Well, I'm trynna change all that."

They rode around the city, sightseeing, jamming to music, getting to know each other better. He told her that he was twenty-four and a widower. When he was eighteen, he married the girl he had been in love with since he was ten years old. She died from breast cancer when she was twenty-two. It was a shock that he still wasn't truly over.

35

"When the doctor first told us, we laughed and told jokes to keep going. We'd joke about how she didn't even have titties for the cancer to attach to. We laughed about how the chemo did her hair a favor and straightened it out. Before chemo, she had some nappy shit." E took a moment and laughed. "But we ran out of stuff to laugh and joke about. That cancer ate her up so fast. She already was skin and bones." He shuddered, as if he was shaking the thoughts away.

"You got any kids?" Jasmine asked him.

"Nah. She was a month pregnant when she found out she had cancer. We had to abort it so she could get treatment. The treatment didn't work. Now I got no baby and no wife."

"I'm so sorry, E."

"Yeah. It actually took me out the streets a minute. But I'm back now."

Jasmine told him that she had been living with her aunt and uncle for the last month. The only thing she really had to look forward to was her seventeenth birthday coming up in about six months. When she said that, he didn't like it.

E told her, "I don't know all the details as to why that's all you got going for you, and I'm glad that you got something to look forward to, but once your birthday gone, then what? What's gonna be your motivation then? What's gonna be your reason to keep living and thriving?"

"Guess I won't have one."

"Find one. ASAP. People out here offing theyself 'cause they claim they ain't got nothing to live for or look forward to. You can't die. Too many books are unread right now."

Jasmine blushed. He seemed to show so much concern and care. "My sisters Michelle and Denise are definitely my reasons to stay around."

"Good. Then I pray that God protects your reasons."

Somewhere in the midst of the conversations and riding and jamming to music, she ended up at his house, in a situation she should have never been in. He was a grown man; she was a child. He knew better. She did, too.

But no matter what the law called it, Jasmine knew she was in love with this man, and she didn't regret it one bit. No matter what the law labeled it, he knew she wasn't the ordinary teenager. He had a thang for her, and he couldn't let her go. He was a complete gentleman. He made her feel comfortable and secure.

"I ain't ready for no relationship, but I'm always here for you, Jasmine. Page me anytime. I'll call you back immediately. It's something about you that I can't leave alone.

Jasmine felt the same way about him.

Chapter 7

"Black! Come on! Let's do our thang!" Wallace called out to Jasmine.

She had been living with her aunt and uncle for three months now. Her hands and wrists weren't sore. She didn't have to hide behind gloves no more.

"How is it staying with Rosalyn and Daniel?" Paw Paw Wallace asked her, as they walked and picked.

"It's better than living at home."

"Really? Okay. One day, you're going to tell me why you really left home."

"I've already told you. I wanted my own room. Sharing a room with Robert was ugh."

Wallace knew that that was a lie. Even though he never went over Shelia's and James's house, he knew that Jasmine did not share a room with Robert. Robert was standoffish and couldn't stand Jasmine. Robert also got whatever he wanted. Ain't no way Robert would have shared a room with Jasmine. Robert would have thrown a fit and called the police if he had to share a room with Jasmine.

"Was James messing with you?"

"No, Sir!"

That question took Jasmine off guard so badly that she had no choice but to answer quickly. If she took too long to answer, Wallace would have read straight through that.

"You sure, Jasmine?"

Wallace never called her Jasmine. She was always Blackberry, Black, or Chocolate Baby Doll. Never Jasmine. That made Jasmine lie even more. She knew that if she told Wallace what James had been doing, she would see a side of her granddad she never wanted to see.

"I'm sure, Paw Paw."

"Them girls of mine love wood more than they own chillen. I love my daughters, but I know that they would stick beside a nigga before sticking beside their own children. And I don't give a damn what Shelia told you. If somebody, anybody, messing with you, you report to me. Ya hear?"

"Yes, Sir."

"Don't let nobody scare you out of saying something. All these Black girls coming up missing, and the news ain't saying shit. These Black girls having babies by family members, and the family ain't saying shit. Black girls—especially dark-skinned girls like you—are treated like gum underneath the desk. White folks treat they dogs better than America treats Black girls—dark-skinned Black girls. But I got you.

"You may be trash to the world, but you are my treasure. So if somebody messing with you, you let me know. I swear to God, Muhammed, Jesus, Moses, Allah, Buddha, John the Baptist, and the angels that they won't mess with you no more."

"Yes, Sir. Thank you, Paw Paw."

"You are loved in this house. Don't let nobody tell you different."

"Nobody could ever tell me different."

"I'll kill me a mothafucka."

"I don't doubt that at all, Paw Paw."

But the concern Jasmine had was that someone would kill *him* if he tried to do something about it. So, she kept it all to herself. She needed her Paw Paw. He was the highlight of her life.

Chapter 8

"Smells good. What are you cooking?" Jasmine asked Rosalyn, as she walked into the kitchen.

"Grits with andouille sausage, smoked gouda cheese, green onions, and bacon in it. Of course some fried chicken on the side. And if I didn't have red Kool-Aid, your uncle would divorce me."

"I can't wait to eat!" Jasmine shrieked.

"I will make sure to fix you double." Rosalyn kissed Jasmine's nose. "I know you're not going to waste it."

"I shole ain't!"

Jasmine had been living with her aunt and uncle for a little over four months. She had gotten so comfortable. She wished she had moved in with them sooner. The house was peaceful. There was no tension nor white elephants in the room that no one was talking about. And she loved their marriage dynamic.

Before observing their marriage, Jasmine never wanted to be married. She'd never witnessed a marriage that made her say, "I want that." Her dad was such a dictator and didn't believe he had to do anything outside of go to work and pay the bills. Her grandmother was too passive and too dedicated to the typical gender roles. Her neighbors didn't believe in typical gender roles enough—the man didn't work at all, and the wife mowed the yard every Saturday and took out the trash every Wednesday.

But Aunt Ros and Uncle D understood what marriage was, in Jasmine's opinion. When they had disagreements, they knew that the enemy was the problem, not each other; they attacked the problem, not each other.

They complemented each other. What one lacked, the other was strong in. When one was leaning, the other held the other up. One washed the dishes and the other dried the dishes. One washed the clothes, the other hung them up. They were a team. Two people working towards a common goal.

Jasmine decided that the next time she saw Paw Paw Wallace, she'd ask him why Daniel doesn't come around the family. And if the reason was because Paw Paw Wallace doesn't like him, then Jasmine had it made up in her mind that she would go to bat for Daniel. She would defend his name. She would tell her Paw Paw all the great things about Daniel that she'd seen with her own eyes.

"Dinner's ready!" Rosalyn called out.

The routine was that Rosalyn would cook, Daniel would set the table, and Jasmine would fix the drinks. Seems simple, but this routine was everything to Jasmine. It meant she was a part of something, she had a role, she was a piece of a puzzle, she was needed, she belonged somewhere, she was a member of a family.

Yes, her grandparents made her feel so loved and whatnot, but she had to leave home to feel that.

Living with her aunt and uncle, she didn't have to leave to feel loved. She felt it right where she was.

"What y'all drinking?" Jasmine asked Rosalyn and Daniel.

"Red Kool-Aid," Daniel answered.

"Water," Rosalyn answered.

"And I'll have a Capri Sun."

Daniel fixed their plates, Jasmine fixed the drinks, and they sat down to eat.

"Last year, you hated geometry, but you came out of there with a B. This year, you hate trigonometry, but you have an A. You do so good even though you hate it. Well, I hate my boss. Help me to hide that fact," Daniel said.

Jasmine laughed. "My advice is just to go to work, make your money, and go home."

"Wise words! Excellent advice. And you're just a kid. You are going to go far, Blackberry," Rosalyn said.

"Thank—," Jasmine began coughing. "you." Jasmine's coughs got deeper and more violent.

"You aighut?" Daniel asked Jasmine.

Jasmine couldn't speak. Her throat was closing in. She grabbed her throat to signal to them that she couldn't breathe.

"Girl, stop playing," Rosalyn said. "Your food gonna get cold."

Jasmine's lips began to swell, and her face broke out in whelps.

"She ain't playing! She's having an allergic reaction!" Daniel yelled, as he ran to a drawer in the kitchen.

Rosalyn continued to eat dinner. Daniel ran back to Jasmine, laid her on the floor, and injected the EpiPen into her right thigh to reverse the allergic reaction. Jasmine took a deep breath of fresh air and vomited.

"Can you talk?" Daniel asked Jasmine once she finished vomiting.

"Yes, I can," Jasmine said, panting.

"Good. If you can talk, then you can breathe. If you can breathe, you can swallow. Drink this."

Daniel gave her liquid diphenhydramine in some red Kool-Aid to keep the allergic reaction from coming back. Jasmine drank it and laid there, getting her thoughts together.

"I didn't know you had an EpiPen," Rosalyn said to Daniel. "I thought you used your last one a few months ago when you ate that peanut butter sandwich."

"I keep these. I got 'em everywhere," Daniel answered.

"Mmph," Rosalyn responded.

"It's good I did. Jasmine woulda died. What the hell happened?!"

"Aunt Rosalyn, did you put shrimp in the grits?"

Rosalyn grabbed her chest in shock. "I am so sorry. I did. I forgot you are allergic."

"That's okay, Auntie. I know you didn't mean to," Jasmine said between gasps.

"Just lay down, Jasmine. Your night is done for." Daniel laughed.

Jasmine got off the floor. "I am so jittery. I don't think I can sleep."

"That's just the side effect of the EpiPen. But that diphenhydramine gonna kick in and knock you on ya ass. Believe me. Go chill out."

"Okay."

Jasmine walked to her room. Daniel looked at Rosalyn suspiciously, and Rosalyn shrugged her shoulders and walked away.

Chapter 9

"What's going—?"

"Shut up! Shut the fuck up!" Daniel told Jasmine, as he covered her mouth with his hand. He forcefully held her down, and she tried to squirm out of his grasp. "You know your aunty tried to kill you, right?"

"No, she didn't," Jasmine defended Rosalyn. "Yeah, she did. She has always hated you. That bitch don't care about you. I saved your life."

Jasmine tried to get out of his stronghold on her.

You better not make a noise because if she comes in here and sees me on top of you, she's gonna kill you for fucking her husband. And I ain't gonna save your life this time. Just lay there like a good girl and let this happen. James already gave me the heads up on you. I'll be quick. You owe me this."

THRUST! Jasmine felt her Uncle Daniel enter her secret place. He didn't have to tell her not to fight him off of her because she had no fight in her left. She was emotionally hurt more than anything. She really trusted him. She really thought she had found her place in this world. She really thought she had a male figure outside of her granddad who would protect her and fight for her.

He was just another man who she needed protection from.

Even if she wanted to fight back, she couldn't. Whatever he put in her Kool-Aid had her dazed and moving in slow motion. Yes, he put diphenhydramine in the red Kool-Aid like he said, but he added something else that only he and God knows. She couldn't even lift her arms, let alone defend herself.

At least he kept his word: he was quick.

"Open your mouth," Daniel demanded Jasmine. She did as told.

He placed a fully loaded Glock in her mouth. "If you say anything to anybody, your brains will be all over Baton Rouge. You got that?"

"Hmm hmm," Jasmine groaned, as tears fell down her cheeks.

Daniel walked out of her room and closed her door.

Am I dreaming? she thought to herself. Diphenhydramine and whatever else made her so sleepy and out of it that she wasn't sure that what had taken place really had taken place. It was really hard to separate reality from delusions. During the accused rape, she was in and out of it, she thought. She just didn't know. She couldn't sort it out in her mind.

"Good morning, Jasmine. How are you?" Rosalyn smiled.

"I'm okay," Jasmine hesitated.

"I am so sorry about yesterday. I am known for my shrimp and grits. I was so excited for you to try

47

it that I forgot you are allergic to seafood. Thank God Daniel had that EpiPen on standby.

"God be looking out, don't He?" Daniel asked. "I'm so glad we ain't planning a funeral! I fixed you a bowl of oatmeal. Only thing in there is sugar and milk."

She must've been dreaming last night. She had to have been caught between two different worlds. Daniel was the same sweet, thoughtful uncle he had always been. That diphenhydramine just had her mentally gone. That had to be it. She put it out of her mind and went to school.

All day at school, her mind was whirring. *Did it or didn't it happen?* Yes, her vagina was sore, but her period would be coming in three days or so. Her vagina was always sore the week of her cycle. She thought extra hard about how she could come to a truthful conclusion about what really happened last night, and she came up blank every time.

"Jasmine!" her biology teacher yelled, getting her attention. "Am I boring you?"

"No, Ma'am."

"Since you are so zoned out, tell me one place hepatitis B is found."

Jasmine gasped.

"Anyone who was paying attention know?" her teacher asked the class.

"Blood," Jasmine answered.

Her teacher was shocked. She thought Jasmine hadn't been paying attention, but she had been.

"That is correct." Her teacher paused. "Appear more with us, if you don't mind."

Her teacher continued teaching the class.

Jasmine had gasped because she knew how she would know if she dreamed the assault or not. She believed that during the time of the assault, she saw that Uncle Daniel had a tattoo of what appeared to be blood drops on his chest. There was no way she would have known that if the sexual assault didn't really happen. She had never seen him with his shirt off before. If she could somehow see his chest, she would know if she dreamt the rape or not.

"You smart as fuck," her classmate John said to her, as they walked out of the classroom into the hallway.

Jasmine had had a crush on John ever since she first laid eyes on him in the ninth grade. They were now in the twelfth grade, and those feelings for him had only intensified. He had never said anything to her; she had never said anything to him. They had never said two words to each other. She didn't even know he noticed her.

She'd always seen him with the slender light skinned girls with "pretty hair". He was a football player who was always surrounded by beautiful girls. Jasmine wasn't sure if she was pretty or not. She just knew that she wasn't light skinned, which was an automatic ugly in most people's books. She didn't have "pretty hair". She put relaxers on her hair which kept it straight. But it was obvious that her straight hair was chemically induced, not natural.

Her natural hair was kinky-curly, not bouncy-curly or juicy-curly or soft and curly. It was dry and nappy, to be frank.

And slender, she was not. She was fat. Period. A size twelve to be exact. Her hips came out beyond her waist. Her butt poked out and could be used as a coaster for drinks. She couldn't suck the bottom of her stomach in, no matter how hard she tried.

Yes, beauty standards were changing, but they would never evolve enough for her to be the "it" girl. No one would ever put her stats in a magazine. Dark skinned, nappy hair, size twelve, wide hips, big butt, huge nose, and a stomach that could be grabbed. It was clear to her that the way she looked would never be beautiful, idolized, or celebrated.

She was far from having low self-esteem. Her granddad made sure of that. She was just realistic. She knew that boys like John would never look her way. So, she enjoyed whatever moment this was that they were experiencing because she knew it would soon be over. *Whenever this ends, at least I still have E,* she thought to herself.

"You think I'm smart? Nah," Jasmine said to John.

"I was watching you all class. You were not paying attention at all. Then she calls you out, and you shut her down with the right answer. You smart as hell."

Wait. Did he say he was watching her all class?

"You were watching me all class?" she asked him.

He smiled at her. His dimples sunk into his face, and his eyes almost disappeared behind his chubby cheeks. "Yeah, I was."

"Why?" She felt herself breathing harder and deeper. She tried to control it, but she was failing at it miserably.

" 'Cause I got a thang for you," he answered her.

She stopped walking and looked at him. His light brown skin was now apple red.

"You do?" she asked him.

"Yeah, I do. Ever since we had geometry last year together. You were smart as hell in that class, too."

Jasmine had no idea what to say or do. But she wasn't going to allow this opportunity to pass her by. "Well, I've been looking at you since we had English together in the ninth grade."

"Word? Okay. Well, are we gonna keep looking at each other, or we gonna do something about it?" John asked her.

"Do something about it." Jasmine blushed.

"Okay, then. Write down your number, and I'll call you tonight."

"I don't know if my aunty and uncle will let that slide."

"Then I'll write down my house number and my pager number. Hit me up tonight, okay?"

"Okay."

John went in his backpack, got out pen and paper, wrote his numbers down, and placed the folded up paper in Jasmine's hand. "Don't lose it."

She placed it in her backpack. "I won't."

They went separate ways to their next class.

Her head was in two different places for the rest of the day: on John and on Uncle Daniel. Her emotions were bipolar. She was ecstatic about John paying her attention and approaching her, but she wasn't sure if she showed it. Her mind was so on wondering if Uncle Daniel had violated her or not that she wasn't sure she gave John the energy he deserved. How would she find out if he had a tattoo on his chest? By the time she was walking home, she had the answer.

"How was school?" Aunt Rosalyn asked her.

"Ugh. It was fine until my English teacher said we had to write an essay on tattoos that our family members have. Of course me and my siblings ain't got no tattoos. Mama and Daddy don't have none. I hope you or Uncle Daniel have one. If not, I'mma have to make some stuff up because Grams shole don't have none, and I don't want to write no paper about them prison tattoos Paw Paw got. How could she make that assignment when not everyone in the world has a tattoo?"

"Well, you lucked up. Between me and your uncle, we have six you can write about. I have a rose on my left breast. I got it because all the girls in college were getting them. Me and my sorority sisters got ours together. No real reason why we got them other than everybody else was getting them.

"For my twenty-first birthday, I got tattoos of wrapped candies going down my left thigh. I did that because I saw an interview where Babyface said he loves candy. He said he always has candy in his pockets, in jars on his desk, in the glove compartment. Just everywhere. I said that if I ever ran into him, I would have an excuse to show him my thigh—because tattoos of candies are on it.

"My third tattoo is—"

"What about Uncle Daniel's tattoos?" Jasmine asked.

She could tell that Aunt Rosalyn was going to go through all of her tattoo stories before getting to Daniel's. Jasmine's anxiety wouldn't let her wait any longer.

"Oh, he's scary. He only has one. And he waited 'til March nineteenth—his birthday—about ten years ago to get it. He was a Blood in the gang, and he was so damn serious about it. He got a tattoo of blood drops on his chest. I never understood gangs. Fighting over streets that don't love you. Beefing with a rival gang who don't mind killing you over turf that don't belong to neither one y'all. Girl. Boy shit."

"Thank you," Jasmine whispered.

"You okay?"

Jasmine cleared her throat. "Yes, Ma'am. I'm going to go write this essay."

"But I didn't tell you about my other tattoos."

"It's just a page and a half assignment. You gave me enough to work with. Thank you."

"Oh."

Jasmine walked to her room, silently shut the door, and cried into a pillow. She cried from the depths of her soul. An outpouring bawl that she couldn't contain, control, or stop.

How could he do this to her? Why would he do this to her? She trusted him, and she never trusted people outside of her grandparents and sisters. She let her guards down for him. She allowed herself to be vulnerable. She allowed him to be closer to her than her own dad. And he did this to her?

She skipped dinner that night. She told Rosalyn it was because she had too much homework to do. But in reality, she didn't want to sit at the table with Rosalyn's perverted husband. The thought of him made her stomach turn. She couldn't digest the truth.

But whether she wanted to admit it or not didn't matter. It happened. And it was about to happen again.

Daniel walked in her room around eleven that night with the same loaded Glock he had the night before. "Open your mouth," he told her. She opened her mouth, and he placed the gun in her mouth, this time further. "You remember what's going to happen if you make a noise or you tell somebody, right?"

Jasmine nodded her head "yes" and laid there like a good girl until he finished.

Chapter 10

"Wow. If you weren't feeling me, that's all you had to say. You ain't have to play me like that yesterday," John said to Jasmine after class.

"I didn't play you. What are you talking about?"

"I waited all night for you to call. I ain't never waited on a chick. But I waited on you. That's cold, Jasmine."

"No! I am so sorry. Family drama last night. I—time just—I'm sorry, John."

"Have a good one, Jasmine."

"No!" Jasmine reached out for him. "I'mma call you tonight. I promise."

"You promise?"

"I promise."

"Okay. I'mma wait. Again."

"My word is bond," she said.

"Nah." John laughed.

"Maybe it wasn't yesterday, but it is today."

"We'll see," he said.

The more Jasmine thought about John, the more her insecurities crept in. He deserved someone better. Someone not damaged. She came with so much baggage. She couldn't even call him last night because she was being raped by her uncle. John deserved to be seventeen and uncaught up in whatever Jasmine had going on.

Word around school was that John was a virgin. If this was true, he really didn't deserve to be caught up in Jasmine's drama. He was living a wholesome, holy, innocent life. She brought the devil with her everywhere she went.

"I get home from football practice at seven tonight, okay?" John said to Jasmine.

"I will call you at seven-o-one," Jasmine said.

"Word."

When Jasmine got home, Aunt Rosalyn and Uncle Daniel were both gone for the night. Daniel was working overnight. Rosalyn was such a mama's girl. She spent the night at her mom's house frequently throughout the week and sometimes slept in the bed with her mom if her dad was working overnight driving trucks. Uncle Daniel and Aunt Rosalyn both being gone for the night was perfect for Jasmine. She could live in peace and sleep in peace.

"Hello?"

"Hi. May I speak to John?"

"May I speak to John?" the voice on the other end of the phone mocked her.

"Gimme the phone, Bigheaded Little Boy!" John yelled. "Jasmine?"

"Yeah, it's me."

"My bad. That's my annoying little brother Justin. And you're late calling me. It's seven-o-two."

"It's seven-o-one on my clock," Jasmine playfully argued.

"Your clock is wrong."

"Prove it."

They stayed on the phone all night long. She found herself in positions she couldn't even explain. Like her feet on the wall, her back on the bed, and her head on the floor while talking to him. He was no better. He found himself twirling the phone cord like a little girl, cheesing from ear to ear talking to her. He had his own phone line, so he didn't have to worry about his parents missing calls.

He had a moment with Jasmine he didn't think he'd ever have. Jasmine was so beautiful to him that he never thought he'd get her. Not only was she beautiful, but she was also smart, had substance, had a personality. All the girls who were in his face only had a face and body to offer; she was the whole package.

Call him crazy, but her chocolate butter skin drove him crazy. He loved her budding curves. He couldn't stand looking at girls who were straight up and down. Jasmine was everything, and she was actually giving him the time of day.

They learned almost everything about each other. They even revealed their darkest secrets to each other. No, she didn't tell him about the rapes from her dad and uncle, but she did tell him that she was afraid of them.

He told her about the thing that kept him up at night. When he was fourteen, his best friend got pregnant by a man who denied the baby and promised he would have nothing to do with the baby. She never told her parents because she was afraid of what they would do to her. She was only thirteen.

John couldn't handle seeing his friend cry day after day, night after night, wondering what she would do to take care of her baby. His fourteen-year-old brain came up with a solution: he told his rich parents that he got her pregnant in hopes that they would take care of their grandchild. But they did quite the opposite. They cursed him for being so stupid, and his mom paid for the abortion without the girl's parents finding out.

The guilt he felt for her getting an abortion weighed so heavily on him that at fourteen, he lost thirty pounds. He told his parents that it wasn't his child, but it was too late. They didn't believe him. They thought he was just saying that to save the baby.

He tried to convince the girl that she did not have to go through with it. His parents had no say over her body. But his friend didn't see any other way out, so she just went with it.

John told Jasmine that it wasn't a second that went by that he didn't think about that unborn child. He said that the abortion eventually broke up his friendship with his friend. Once the reality of what she had done set in, she was so angry and furious at John for involving his parents that she never acknowledged him again.

"Have you ever gotten a girl pregnant?" Jasmine asked him.

" No. I'm a virgin."

"Why?"

"Waiting on the girl who's worth it. So much comes with sharing your body with someone else. She gotta be worth it."

Jasmine felt like the trash that she saw herself as once she found out that he was a virgin. She wasn't *not* a virgin by choice. Before E, she had never voluntarily had sex, but it all amounted to the same results: she was busted wide open. Her seal had been broken. She was tainted. It was nothing to have sex with E. Not like she was a virgin anyway. What exactly did she have to look forward to and wait on?

When he asked if she was a virgin, she hesitantly said, "No." He was far from slow or sheltered. He didn't know the details, but her slowness to answer let him know that she didn't lose her virginity by her own free will. He wasn't going to press her into saying anything. When she was ready, she would talk. He was just enjoying her presence and aura. Whatever she had been through didn't matter to him. He had her. That was the hard part. Now he had to keep her—that was the hardest part.

"It's one in the morning, John. We gotta go to bed."

"Hang up, then."

"No, you hang up."

"On three, hang up."

Neither one ever hung up. They fell asleep on the phone. When she woke up, she silently panicked. Her thoughts were so intrusive: *Was I snoring? Did I grind my teeth in my sleep? Did I sleep talk? Did I grunt?*

Her alarm clock going off woke him up a few seconds after it woke her up.

"Why is your alarm going off at five thirty?" he asked, groggily.

"I walk to school. And once I get to school, I take a bird bath in the bathroom's sink to freshen back up."

"I thought you rode Mr. Rogers' bus."

"I did when I lived with my mom and dad. I live with my aunty and uncle now, remember?"

"Yeah, I remember. I just didn't know you had to walk. Damn. Well, I'll see you in third period."

"Okay. Bye."

"Uh uh. Don't tell me bye. Say, 'See you later.' "

"See you later, John."

They both hung up.

They smiled at each other all third period. He walked her to classes when he could. He read her body language. She was guarded. He respected all of her limits and boundaries. She didn't welcome physical touch, so holding her hand was out of the question. But she definitely allowed time and non-physical affection.

"So, you my girl or what?" he asked her after school.

"Are you going to ask me or what?"

"No. Because if you say no, I'mma be too embarrassed."

"If you don't ask me, I'mma be too pissed," she replied.

"Aah! I ain't never done this before, so give me a pass if I fuck it up."

"Yeah, yeah. Come on with it."

"Jasmine LaBrea Hines, will you please be my girl?"

"Nope!"

John's face dropped.

"I am playing with you. Yes, I will."

"Whew. You play too damn much."

She held her fist out for a dap. It took him off guard a little bit, but he knew that was to be expected. She didn't feel safe enough with him yet to be physical in any kind of way. He expected a hug and wanted a kiss. But he dapped her up and made note to respect her timing and pace. She reminded him not to call her because her uncle would be home, and they went on their way.

She thought about E a lot. She was really into him, but not the way she was into John. Besides, E told her that he wasn't ready for a girlfriend. She knew that that meant he was seeing other girls besides her. She wanted somebody to herself. Someone she didn't have to share. John was that somebody.

E was also in the streets. He tried to hide the guns and drugs from her, but he wasn't good at it.

He could hide things from the police, but he couldn't hide things from her. She was a better investigator than the FBI.

She noticed the nickel bags taped underneath the kitchen table. She saw the brick of cocaine in the back of the TV that he never turned on. She saw all the guns behind his suits in the closet. She ran across the money he had in an ice cream bucket in the freezer. His car tint was illegal in every state and every country.

She was well aware of what was going on, and she wanted no parts of it. He was an itch that she scratched. It was time to move on.

Chapter 11

John hated feeling feminine in any way. He was a man's man. All things masculine were him: sports, tattoos, hairy body, weight lifting, barbecuing, fixing things, wrestling with his boys, etcetera. But Jasmine made him soft. Not soft by the world's definition, but soft by his own belief.

He internally felt like he was skipping when he walked. She had him twirling his hair whenever he talked to her. He showed all thirty-two teeth whenever he smiled. Before her, he didn't even smile. He grinned or smirked. But a full-blown smile? No, Ma'am, no, Sir. Most people didn't even know he had dimples because he never did anything to reveal him. But Jasmine had him smiling deep and talking loud.

He felt his facial cheeks get hot whenever she ran across his mind. He found himself doodling her name on random pieces of paper and drawing hearts with her name in it. He wrote his and her names across every last one of his composition notebooks.

All the things that he considered cheesy and teased his homeboys about when they were feeling a chick, he was doing. He now understood the stupidity and bliss that love brought. Love makes you so stupid that you don't care who's watching, who's talking, who's thinking what. You're just gonna stick beside them, and whoever doesn't like it, well, that's their problem.

John didn't believe in being with someone your parents and/or closest friends didn't approve of. Well, he didn't before he got with Jasmine. Before getting with her, in his mind, you couldn't have a successful, happy relationship without the stamp of approval of your family and friends. But once he got with Jasmine, he said fuck their stamps of approval. She made him happy. The end. Their opinions literally didn't matter. What they thought about Jasmine and him being together had no effect on him. That was his girl, and he was going to stick beside her.

As soon as he went home after school, he told his parents about her. For his mom, the first red flag about her was her name.

"Jasmine? I bet she's fast. You better watch her. You know the jasmine flower is known to increase sexual desires in people. It is also known for its intoxicating, alluring scent. All she's gonna do is seduce you and lead you astray," John's mom said to him.

"You act like she named herself."

"Something led whoever named her to name her that. They saw it on her. Be careful. You know how you get with girls."

"I don't get no type of way with girls. What are you talking about?"

"Do I need to remind you about that fiasco that we had to pay to go away?"

"Oh, my God, Mama. Really? I was fourteen. I loved my friend and wanted the best for her. I acted and spoke without considering the consequences. Call the sheriff."

"We're not having that again."

"Okay, Mama."

"And what do her parents do for a living?"

"Her mom is a dispatcher. Her dad works at a plant."

"So they both stink."

"Wanda!" his dad called out to her mom. "Stop it. They may be poor, but that doesn't mean they stink. Soap is not expensive."

"Who said they were poor?" John asked.

His dad chuckled. "Son. Her mom is a dispatcher. And her dad works at a plant? I mean, if he owned it, that'd be one thing. But he works there. Ummm…"

"Sounds to me like she has two parents who know how to work hard and handle bills by any means necessary," John defended.

"Sounds to me like you're dating a charity case. Don't call us when she starts needing the basic necessities," his mom stated.

The truth was that his mom saw how his face lit up whenever he talked about Jasmine. His face never lit up for anyone. Not even a few years ago when he talked about the girl who he'd gotten pregnant. She didn't like the idea of some hussy coming along, snatching her baby away from her. John was her most prized possession. Who did this Jasmine think she was? She was going to find everything wrong with Jasmine until John called it quits with her. Wanda couldn't dare risk losing her baby to… to… *that.*

His dad just believed that everyone was beneath him. He came from literally nothing and climbed through dirt, mud, and grit to becoming the district attorney. In his eyes, no one had an excuse to have less than. He went from living under a bridge to having a closet for every day of the week.

While he was broke in law school, he found ways to put his wife through law school right along with him. She became a judge three days before he became a D.A. No one was on their level. No one was even worthy of speaking to them, let alone date their boys. Whoever this riff raff Jasmine was, was going to have to find her own place on this earth to beg, borrow, and steal because she wasn't going to be doing it to them.

"And what does she look like?" his mom asked him.

"Beautiful. Inside and out," was John's simple reply.

"That means she's ugly," Justin told Wanda.

"How?!" John asked.

His dad answered, "When a girl is fine, you say shit like, 'Man, she's bad! She got a body! Her hair comes down her back. Her skin looks like it's been kissed by the sun.' When a girl ugly, you say shit like, 'She's a child of God.' "

"Or, 'She's beautiful. Inside and out,' " his mother added.

John shook his head. He was mad with himself for ever believing that he could share a moment with his parents. If it wasn't about trophies or money or anything shiny they could show off, they didn't care.

There was no way he'd tell them that she was dark-skinned and chubby. Their beauty standards were simple: light, bright, and damn near White with no waistline. For people who hated White people, they sure wanted to be them and wanted their sons to end up with them damn near. The horror he'd put his parents through letting them know that his girlfriend couldn't pass a paper bag test was unmeasurable, so he didn't.

"All I know is she better not be dark-skinned. Yo' Black ass barely made it out light brown. Get with a darkie, and our grandbabies will have hell the rest of their lives. That'd mean we'd have to cover them up whenever we take them out in public. One, so people won't see their dark, tainted, flawed skin. Two, so that they won't get darker. Because one thang about dark people, they gone get darker," his dad said.

"If they are dark-skinned, I'm not babysitting, John. I don't need the stress of having to lug around a darkie. You created the monster, you find the solution," his mom stated.

"At least with that girl you got pregnant, she was light-skinned with good hair. At least you got that part right," his dad added.

The thing that John couldn't understand was how either one of them could feel that way. His dad was light-skinned, and his mom was dark-skinned. How couldn't they understand if he had fallen in love with a dark-skinned girl? How couldn't the mom feel proud and honored that he had gotten with a girl who reminded him of her? Didn't she love her damn self?!

It ain't like you're the prettiest yo' damn self. You shole as hell ain't the skinniest. And yo' Blickity Black ass got the nappiest hair I've ever seen. And you got the nerve to have high standards for your future daughter in laws. Where are your standards for your own ugly, Black, fat ass?! You halfway look like you belong on the plantation trying to find freedom with Harriet Tubman, John thought to himself.

And when he told his football player friends… shit really hit the fan.

"Nigga, you got a reputation to maintain. You get with Crispy?"

"You making us all look bad. We are known for baggin' and smashin' the baddest. What the fuck is you doing? Blackie? Really?"

"Of all the bitches in this school, that's the best you can do?"

"You got hoes on yo' jock every damn second. And that's the route you go?!"

At least his friend Royce had something nice to say. "Mane, lift her stomach up and hit that pussy.

That belly ain't doing nothing but keeping that pussy warm for you."

"That pussy burnt! Couldn't be me!"

"And it ain't you," John said. "None of y'all gotta like it. But you will respect it. And when you see her, treat her like you treat the rest of the girlfriends. She ain't did shit to none of y'all."

"Mane, none of our girlfriends gonna hang with Smut. She can't pass for a cheerleader, a dancer… Only thing she can pass for is a wide receiver. The same way we got a reputation to maintain, our girls do, too. We can't be seen with her, and they can't, either."

"She ain't trynna be seen with y'all. She got her own mind. She outta y'all league. I ain't saying hang with her. I said respect her. Look out for her. Make sure she good. Like y'all do the other girlfriends."

"What you trynna prove by being with her?" his best friend Damien asked him.

"I ain't got shit to prove. I love her. That's that."

Truthfully, all the football players had a thing for her one way or another. They just weren't as bold as John to admit it or pursue her. She was so damn beautiful. She looked like she was drawn and painted by Leonardo di Vinci. They didn't know what the big deal about Mona Lisa was, but Jasmine was definitely a work of art that needed to be displayed. They couldn't bring themselves to admit that a dark-skinned chubby girl had their attention, but she did.

It was confusing to them. They didn't understand how or why. Was she changing the beauty standards? Was she the prototype? How could they be attracted to a girl who was dark-skinned *and* chubby? How did she have two things working against her, and she still be so damn pretty?

Chapter 12

Since they couldn't go to bed on the phone together the night before, Jasmine decided to surprise John before school at football practice Friday morning. She had made him an egg sandwich—his favorite.

"Midnight, John ain't here," one of the football players said to Jasmine. "It's his birthday. Coach took him out to breakfast."

Five of the football players began walking towards her.

"I don't know what John sees in yo' Black ass. Must be the pussy," another football player said.

"Hell, yeah. Gotta be."

They continued to walk towards her.

"I'm just gonna go," Jasmine said.

"Uh uh. Bring yo' ass back."

Jasmine began to walk faster. The faster she walked, the faster the players walked.

Jasmine threw the egg sandwich down and began running across the field. She made it to the bleachers before Damien, the quarterback, grabbed her and threw her down underneath the bleachers. Damien was the ladies' man. No girl ever told him no. His build, looks, personality, everything made him the most wanted boy on campus.

He always walked around with a disposable camera either in his backpack or in his hand because he was going to be a famous photographer one day. The girls always would walk up to him and ask him to take pictures of them by themselves or with him. Jasmine never did. She never gave him any energy. He couldn't stand her because of that.

He had no idea why Jasmine didn't want him like the other girls did. He couldn't accept that she wanted John over him. John was always the girls' second pick when they couldn't get Damien. How dare Jasmine be different?

"Hold your ass still. If you don't fight it, it'll be over quicker," Damien told her.

Four of them held her down underneath the bleachers and ripped her panties off her. She mentally began beating herself up for wearing a dress. She wanted to look good for John; she didn't know that it would be an invitation to be raped.

She fought as much as she could. She just wasn't a match for five burly football players. They strangled her and held her down by her wrists as their body weight anchored her torso. They each took a turn on her. After the second guy, she saw no use in fighting anymore. She laid there and let it happen.

"She stopped crying and screaming. She must like it." Damien laughed.

"This fat bitch like this shit," another player said.

Once they all had their turn, they all headed back to the field, dapping each other up. Jasmine remained under the bleachers getting herself together. The tears found their way back to her face.

This can't be real. This can't be my life story. Is every girl going through this? Why me? Almost every man in my life? Really? It has to be me. I must be the problem.

After about twenty minutes of Jasmine trying to get herself together underneath the bleachers, John made it to the field. He didn't see Jasmine, but Jasmine saw him. She heard bits and pieces of the players' conversation.

"Happy birthday, Kid. You know we gone do it up this weekend," Damien said.

"Fa sho'."

"Where's Coach?" Chris asked.

"He stopped by the locker room. He coming," John answered.

"Your girl came by here," Damien said.

"Really?" John's face lit up. He loved him some Jasmine, and everyone knew that.

"Yeah. She came through with a dress on, trying to fuck all of us. We shut that down, though."

"No, she didn't," John said, in disbelief.

"Yeah, Bro. She did. I been telling you she a hoe and you need to leave her alone. She ain't no good. My mama said bitches that black ain't nothing but snakes and devils. She one way in your face and another way behind your back. Leave her alone, Bro," Damien said.

John's face slowly crumbled. It was hard for him to believe that, especially when they had never had sex or even got close to having sex. They never even had the conversation about sex. She was guarded and reserved. She barely let him hold her hand. Ain't no way she tried to have sex with five boys she didn't know. John wasn't going for that.

He was slowly realizing these weren't his friends. They had been together since middle school. He and Damien had been friends since elementary. But it was clear they were all reaching the end of their roads with John. When he told them to respect Jasmine, he meant that. And respecting her meant not lying on her or calling her things that she wasn't. He didn't know what the problem was they had with her, but he really didn't care to find out. They had crossed the line.

Jasmine internally pleaded with John to not believe them. She wanted to run from underneath the bleachers and show him what they did. She wanted to show him her torn panties. She wanted to show him her tear-stained face. She wanted to yell to the mountaintops all that she'd endured since she was nine years young. But the shame of being damaged and ruined grabbed her tongue. She decided to let John believe whatever he wanted to believe. She had no more fight in her. At all.

Chapter 13

Back to E she went. She knew it was over between she and John. At this point, she didn't even want to be with him anymore. He deserved so much better. He didn't need to get caught up in whatever curse was on her life. He was headed for greatness, and she felt that she would hinder all that.

She paged E. He called her, and she asked him to pick her up from the library. She wanted to just ride and lose herself in whatever music he would play. He had the perfect car to ride in because his windows were so dark that they looked painted black. No one could tell Aunt Rosalyn and Uncle Daniel that they saw her riding around town with a grown man. And he always picked her up in the back of the library where no one could see them.

"I brought your juicy self a burger," E told her, as she was getting inside his car.

"I could cry. Thank you!"

"You welcome. I knew you were gonna be hungry. Wassup? You good?"

She didn't answer him. She just ate her burger as he drove.

"I got some people who will handle whatever you need to be handled," he told her after twenty minutes of silence. "Just tell me where they need to assimilate at."

Jasmine thought long and hard about that offer. Getting rid of those football players and her uncle and her dad would literally give her a new life. But she wasn't a murderer nor a hit man nor one to conspire. She decided to just let it ride and let God deal with them.

"God got it," Jasmine answered him.

"Shiiid. God can't handle it the way I can. Belee dat. If you ever get tired of waiting on Big Homie in the sky, you got my beeper."

They ended up riding to New Orleans and back. An approximately two-hour drive.

"I can drop you up the street from your house, and you walk home. It's too dark to be walking from the library."

"Yeah. That's fine."

E dropped her off at the stop sign up the street from Aunt Rosalyn's and Uncle Daniel's house.

"Thank you for today," she said to him.

"Anytime. Maybe you'll talk next time."

"Maybe."

When she got back home, Aunt Rosalyn looked at her and smiled. "John called here for you."

Jasmine's face lit up. "Really?!"

"A thousand times. And he said it was urgent. Who is John?"

Aunt Rosalyn didn't seem mad at all. She seemed excited that her niece had a young man of interest. Rosalyn was silently starting to worry that Jasmine was gay. Jasmine didn't wear makeup and showed no interest in doing so. She didn't dress the girliest. Even when she was in a dress or skirt, it was wearing her instead of her wearing it. The last thing her dark-skinned, chubby self needed was to be gay.

"John goes to my school. He asked me to be his girlfriend. I said yes."

"Aaahhh!" Aunt Rosalyn shrieked. "Okay. Well, we got to meet him. He ain't gonna just be courtin' you and never meet the family. He gotta know that you got a team behind you that is down for whatever. He needs to know that you have a family who loves you and won't let him do anything to you.

"I am excited for you, though. This your first real boyfriend?"

Jasmine nodded her head "yes".

"I remember mine. I was younger than you, though. Shoot, I was thirteen. But it was a different time back then. Anyways, he sounds nice. I can't wait to meet him, and I won't tell your parents."

"Thank you."

Jasmine thought that it was over between she and John. She thought that he wanted nothing to do with her after his friends told him that she was trying to have sex with them all. But according to Aunt Rosalyn, he blew their phone up trying to get to her. You don't call somebody a thousand times that you want nothing to do with. You don't call anybody that you hate that much.

Or do you?

Her mind began playing tricks on her. What if he was calling to yell? To break up with her? To tell her that he believed his teammates?

Her excitement quickly turned to butterflies in her stomach and nerves in her throat. She decided to not call him. She would face that situation demon Monday.

She avoided answering the phone all weekend. She couldn't risk answering the phone and it be him. She wished that Aunt Rosalyn and Uncle Daniel had money to buy a caller id. That would have erased this problem.

She told Aunt Rosalyn to always tell him she wasn't home. Rosalyn couldn't understand why she was avoiding John. She had seen the way Jasmine's face lit up when she talked about him. What was the problem?

"I don't want to talk about it," Jasmine told Aunt Rosalyn when she questioned her about avoiding John.

"Well, how long am I supposed to keep lying to the little boy? He sounds like a sick puppy dog."

"I don't know for how long. But definitely this weekend."

"Okay, Jasmine. If you say so."

Daniel never answered the phone. He said no one ever called for him, so why answer a phone? When he found out Jasmine had a boyfriend, he didn't care. After assaulting her six times, he vowed to never touch her again anyway. She had caused a problem in his marriage.

Chapter 14

Jasmine thought that she would face the situation in biology class when she saw John, but John was waiting for her on the sidewalk leading up to the school Monday morning.

"Why are you avoiding me?" he asked her.

"I just had a bad weekend."

"Jasmine. I feel like I'm constantly chasing you. You ain't the same every day. I never know which Jasmine I'mma get. Am I gonna get the Jasmine who is in love with me? Am I gonna get the Jasmine who wants to be left alone? Am I gonna get the Jasmine who can't get enough of me? This shit is tiring. You want me or not? You want this or not? 'Cause I want you, and I want this."

Jasmine felt so much relief to hear him say that. So, he wasn't calling her all weekend to break up with her. He really was calling just to talk.

"You still want me?" she asked him.

"Yes! Why would you ask me that?"

"Why were you calling me all weekend?"

"To talk to my girl. What you mean?"

"Anything in particular?"

"Yeah. A lot in particular. You my best friend. I tell you everything. I really wanted to tell you how them niggas on the team so damn jealous of me and you that they claim you tried to have sex with them." John laughed. "I know you. Ain't no way.

They just mad that I got something that nobody else can have."

It felt as if a weight was removed from her chest; the elephant had left the room.

"They said what?" Jasmine asked, trying to sound shocked.

"Right. I ain't sweating that. That ain't even how you get down."

"At all. What else you wanted to tell me?"

They had begun walking to school.

"I beat a level on Mortal Kombat I been trying to beat for months."

"What?! Finally. Who were you when you beat it?"

"I don't wanna tell you." John shook his head.

"Oh! So you were Blaze. I told you being Raiden wasn't gonna get it!"

"Yeah, yeah." He lovingly waved her off.

"What else you wanted to tell me?"

"I ain't telling you. You shoulda answered that phone or called me back. Why you be disappearing like that?"

Jasmine shrugged her shoulders.

"You do know. And you never answered my questions. Do you still want me, and do you still want this?"

"Yes, and yes."

"Then act like it. Don't pull that no mo'."

"You're right. I'm sorry. And I'm sorry I missed your birthday. You didn't tell me that it was your birthday, number one. I went to see you that morning at football practice, and they told me Coach took you somewhere for your birthday breakfast. Number two, I had a bad weekend. I am sorry I missed it. What did you do?"

"Nothing. Nothing at all. I waited by the phone all weekend waiting on you to call. That's how I ended up with so much time to beat a level on Mortal Kombat."

"I am so sorry, John. Your eighteenth birthday, and I ruined it."

"You could never ruin anything. Why was your weekend bad?"

She had mentally drained herself so badly thinking about what John was calling her about. She had created so many scenarios in her head that it made her body limp. She literally made herself sick over the weekend thinking that she had lost John. If only she had picked up the phone, she would have saved herself the sickness, and John would have enjoyed his eighteenth birthday celebration weekend.

"Nothing. Sometimes my thoughts just take off. Nothing happened. Don't worry about it," she answered John.

"Next time, before your thoughts take you on a ride, call me. I can hop in a passenger seat, too."

As much as Jasmine wanted John, she couldn't fight the guilt she had about being assaulted by his teammates. She knew it wasn't her fault and that she did nothing wrong, but she never told John, and that was eating away at her. She wondered if she should tell him because he really thought Damien was his best friend. She wondered if she should have told him the type of "friends" he really had. She also wondered if raping girls were their thing, including John's.

You *are* the company you keep. So was John a rapist, too? Did he undervalue women? Did he feel that no girl was supposed to tell him no, and if they did, sexual assault was the consequence? Was he as big of a monster as the rest of his teammates?

But one look in his eyes, she could tell that he was different. He wasn't a monster or demon. He was a regular eighteen-year-old boy who worried about making it big and having a girlfriend. He was the exception to the company he kept.

Chapter 15

"I got a boyfriend," Jasmine told Michelle, all giddy-like.

"I knew something was different about you! You look so… happy!"

"He makes me so happy, Michelle!"

"What's his name?"

"John."

"John? That's an old man name."

"He can't help what his parents named him."

"What does he look like?"

"Like he's straight out of *GQ* magazine."

"What's *GQ* magazine?"

"Nothing." Jasmine laughed to herself, remembering Michelle was only eleven years old. If it wasn't baby dolls or playing in their mom's high heel shoes, it went over her head.

"What does John look like? Do his eyes sparkle like the stars? Does his skin shine under the sun? Does his voice sound like God?"

As childish as her questions were, the answers were "yes" to them all.

"Yeah, Michelle."

"Ooh! Does he look like Dwayne Wayne from *A Different World*?"

"No! He looks like Romeo from Immature."

"Ugh. Romeo looks like a girl. You like girls?"

"Hell no!" Jasmine yelled. "My life ain't that damn bad. Antyways, John is my everything. After God."

"I got a boyfriend, too," Michelle whispered.

"What?! You are a kid! You're only ten years old!"

"I turned eleven last week, remember?"

"Yeah, whatever. Still a kid."

"And? I won't tell nobody you got a boyfriend if you don't tell nobody I have a boyfriend."

Jasmine sighed. Blackmail at its finest. But Jasmine agreed because she was sure that at eleven, they weren't doing anything but coloring pictures and changing her Baby Alive doll's diapers. How serious could it really be? Nothing to get her in trouble over.

"Okay. Who is this boyfriend? Do his eyes sparkle like the stars? Does his skin shine under the sun? Does his voice sound like God?" Jasmine asked, mocking Michelle from earlier.

"No. I don't want to be his girlfriend, but he said that I am. And that I better not tell anybody."

"Who is it, Michelle?" Jasmine began to get worried.

"Robert," Michelle whispered.

"Our brother?" Jasmine asked.

Michelle nodded her head "yes". Jasmine's stomach began to churn, and underneath her skin became fire hot. She knew she had to remain calm. If she would have become irate, Michelle would shut down and stop talking. She didn't need her to do that.

"How is he your boyfriend? What things do you do together?"

"He buys me ice cream after school. He kisses my cheek. And he—" Michelle pointed to between her legs.

Jasmine swallowed a lump in her throat. "What does he do there?"

"He puts his wee wee in mine. And sometimes he puts his wee wee in my mouth."

"Okay, Michelle. We have to tell Paw Paw, okay?"

"No! Robert would be so mad! I promised I wouldn't tell. You promised you wouldn't tell! No!"

"Michelle—"

"I keep all your secrets, Jasmine. I even kept the secrets night after night when I would see Dad leave your room. You owe me!"

Jasmine took a minute and realized how afraid Michelle must have been. She knew that Michelle had to be afraid because she was, too. She had never told anyone about her dad or her uncle or the football players raping her; was it fair to expect Michelle to tell someone?

She also realized that her silence about her own situation made Michelle feel that it was fine to keep silent about hers. Jasmine knew that she was the older sister and that her sisters were watching her, seeing how to walk, how to talk, how to react, if to react, etcetera. She failed Michelle.

"Michelle, we have to say something."

"You never told anybody. Why I have to?"

"It's different."

"How?! Explain to me!" Tears flowed down Michelle's face.

"You're right. It's not different. I'm not going to say anything. But tell him that you know that it's wrong and that you won't do it no more."

"But he buys me ice cream."

"Dammit, Michelle, I will buy you ice cream! You don't have to go along with his bullshit! And you won't! No more, okay?"

"Okay," Michelle whispered.

"I mean it. Promise me."

"I promise."

Chapter 16

Jasmine prayed all night while Michelle was asleep. She knew that something had to be done about Robert. Robert was entitled his whole damn life. His parents never held him accountable for anything. He was their golden child—literally and figuratively. He was light-skinned, and his hue appeared gold. Also, he was their only boy.

James only wanted a boy. He didn't want any girls. Jasmine was the mistake. She was their first child, and they didn't get it right. Their next child—Robert—was their redemption. Since James loved Robert so much and worshipped the ground he walked on, that made Shelia worship the ground Robert walked on as well. Whatever her husband said and did, she followed suit.

Paw Paw and Grams tried to intervene in the beginning. When it was just normal child temper tantrums, they tried to stop it there, but Shelia always told them to mind their own business. "Y'all raised y'all children. Just be the grandparents and let me raise my own damn kids."

When it got to the point of Robert realizing he didn't have to respect anything or anybody, so he didn't, Paw Paw and Grams stopped allowing him at their house. "If I can't discipline the child, the child can't be at my house where I pay the motherfucking bills," Paw Paw said.

Robert had destroyed his grandparents' house when he was eight years old. He pulled the curtains down and broke a dresser mirror because Grams told him that he couldn't have a fifth cookie. Paw Paw immediately put a belt on his ass for the damage he had done. Robert told his mom as soon as she picked him up from his grandparents' house.

All hell broke loose. Shelia cursed her dad out for whipping him, and she cursed her mama out for allowing it to happen. She also yelled at her mama for telling Robert that he couldn't have five cookies. "It's your fault all this happened in the first place. If you woulda just let him have the cookie, none of this would have happened!"

That was five years ago. Robert hadn't been allowed back at their house since. Grams would still send Robert birthday and Christmas presents at first, but Shelia told her that Robert didn't want shit from her. Paw Paw told Grams to save her money and stop sending his ungrateful, disrespectful ass things. Grams wasn't built like that. She bought strangers things for holidays; how could she not buy her own grandson something? But the sting lessened as the years went by, and it stopped bothering her after a while.

Robert never called to check on his grandparents. The grandparents moved on as if they didn't have a grandson. And that became the norm.

With Robert never having to be accountable for his actions, and with everything he did being acceptable according to his parents, it was only a matter of time before Robert took after his dad and became a predator. The time was now.

Jasmine tossed and turned all night, thinking of what she could do or say to stop this. She had to keep her word with Michelle. But she also had to protect her. Protecting her also meant lying sometimes. They were at their grandparents' house. It would have been nothing for Jasmine to wake Paw Paw up and tell him what Robert had done to Michelle. It would take nothing for her to call the police. It was so simple as SAYING SOMETHING, but she just couldn't do it. She also couldn't just sit back and allow her sister to be raped.

Michelle heard Jasmine tossing and turning all night. Jasmine's disturbed spirit wouldn't allow Michelle to rest.

"I got it. Trust me. It won't happen again," Michelle told Jasmine in the middle of the night. "Go to sleep. I got this."

There was something about the way Michelle said it. The assurance and security in her voice. Jasmine knew that Michelle would handle it. She felt it. She let it go and went to sleep.

Chapter 17

"Jasmine!" Rosalyn called out. "Michelle is here!"

Jasmine ran to the living room after hearing the franticness in her Aunt Rosalyn's voice. Jasmine saw a battered and bruised Michelle.

"Michelle!" Jasmine yelled.

"She won't say what happened," Daniel said.

"How did you get here?" Jasmine asked her.

"I ran."

"You ran all the way from Mama and Daddy's house?"

Michelle nodded her head "yes".

"Let's go to my room."

Michelle and Jasmine walked to Jasmine's room. Jasmine made sure to close the door and lock it. She turned the music up extra loud so no one could hear what was being said.

"What happened, Shelley?"

Jasmine called Michelle Shelley whenever she wanted to calm her down and gain her trust.

"I did what you told me to do. I told Robert no. I told him it was wrong, and we couldn't do that anymore. He beat me up really bad, Jasmine. He was so big and fast. I tried to fight him back, but I couldn't." Michelle sobbed uncontrollably.

Jasmine held her and consoled her the best way she could.

"I am so sorry this happened to you, Shelley."

90

"Now he's mad at me. He probably hates me. He probably doesn't love me no more. He probably will never speak to me again. And this is your fault!"

"Shelley, he never loved you. Anyone who loves you wouldn't do that to you."

"So Dad doesn't love you?"

"No, he doesn't."

"Uncle Daniel doesn't love you, either?"

That comment took Jasmine off guard. "What? What do you mean?"

"I heard Daddy and Uncle Daniel at Grams and Paw Paw's house talking about how they do what they do to you."

Jasmine swallowed her emotions. "You're right. Daddy and Uncle Daniel don't love me, either. Who did you tell that you heard that conversation?"

"Nobody. Because we hold each other's secrets. Right?"

Jasmine hesitated. She thought long and hard about what Michelle was saying. Jasmine knew that if she told someone about what Robert had been doing to Michelle, Michelle would tell what their dad and uncle had been doing to her. She didn't want to betray Michelle's trust, but she also needed to protect her. But then she thought about it. No one was going to protect Michelle if she said something.

Their grandma would just sing and pray about it. Their mama would just kick Michelle out of the house the way she kicked her out of the house.

91

Rosalyn would probably rejoice because she was so bitter about not being able to have kids that she hated all children, especially her sister's. Daniel would high-five Robert. Their dad was probably the one who groomed Robert to be the predator that he was.

Paw Paw Wallace would be the only one to do something. But Paw Paw Wallace wasn't wrapped too tight. He believed in pulling the trigger on anybody who crossed someone he loved. He wouldn't care that Robert was a child. Robert had to die. And if he hurt Robert, Shelia and James would come after him because Robert was their golden child. Jasmine was not going to put her beloved Paw Paw in that position.

"Spend the night tonight. We have to think of something to tell Mama and Daddy. They're going to want to know why you're over here. And when they see you, they're going to want to know what happened to you. But we'll think of something tomorrow. Go to bed, okay?"

"What if Uncle Daniel does to me what he does to you?"

"He won't!" Jasmine yelled. I will kill him before he even touches your hand." And she meant that.

"Okay."

Jasmine found Daniel in the kitchen. Rosalyn was outside on the phone.

"You will not touch Michelle. At all." Jasmine spoke with much authority. "I will kill you. The end."

Her tone let Daniel know that she wasn't playing. He wasn't going to test her. He agreed to her statement.

It had been two months since he last sexually assaulted Jasmine. Jasmine didn't know why he stopped, but she thanked God that he did.

"And I won't allow you to touch me ever again, either. You got that?"

"Yeah."

Jasmine and Michelle slept the night away peacefully.

Chapter 18

Two months ago, Rosalyn noticed that Daniel's sex drive had been down. That was a red flag because Daniel and Rosalyn were usually at it like rabbits. They went from having sex twice every day to having sex twice a week. Rosalyn questioned him about it, and his answer blew her mind.

"Since you ain't gone let up, I'mma let you know. And, Baby, I'm sorry. I have no excuses. I tried to resist her. But she kept at it. Every time your back was turned, anytime you were at work, every time you were far away. I'm a man. After so many times, a man gets weak. I was born with only so many 'no's' in me. I ran out of no's," Daniel told Rosalyn.

"Who is she, Daniel?"

Daniel was silent for a minute or two. Rosalyn patiently waited for him to break.

"Jasmine."

"Jasmine who?! My niece Jasmine? My sister's child Jasmine?"

"Yes," he whispered, with his head down.

Rosalyn quivered on the inside. She didn't know how to feel nor how to react. She knew Jasmine was a child. But Daniel had never done anything like this before. Jasmine had to have been the problem.

"That li'l girl is fast, Rosalyn."

Rosalyn nodded her head, allowing every thought to have its moment.

"That's why she got kicked out of her mama and daddy house. 'Cause she fast as hell. Hot in the ass. She's a problem."

Rosalyn heard everything that he said. And it may have been true. But she was still just a… child. Daniel was an adult. He was supposed to say no, walk away. This wasn't acceptable.

"But that's statutory rape, Daniel. She's a child!"

"You don't think I know that?! But she's persistent. She won't let me lone 'bot it."

"This ain't right." Rosalyn shook her head, panting hard.

"Hell, you the one who tried to kill her! You knew she was allergic to shrimp, but you diced it up real small to where she wouldn't notice and fed it to her anyway. That wasn't right, either. We both have had our fun with her."

Rosalyn couldn't think of anything to say. He was right. They'd both had their way with Jasmine.

"We both could go to jail for what we did," Daniel added.

"You're right."

"So let's just let it ride. You don't tell on me; I don't tell on you."

"But I did what I did one time. Only God knows how many times y'all have done what you did."

"It don't matter. You were still wrong, Rosalyn."

"Okay! Don't do it no more. Break up with her. Let's just both act like nothing ever happened on our end."

"Cool."

Daniel had dirt on Rosalyn. Rosalyn couldn't say anything or judge Daniel. She was stuck between feeling like Daniel was a pedophile and Jasmine was fast. She was stuck between seeing her niece as a victim and seeing her niece as the pursuer.

She decided to pray about how she perceived her niece Jasmine. She was going to pray it away. Her husband made a mistake. That's to be expected when another female enters the home. In a way, Daniel was the victim. He was placed into temptation involuntarily. Rosalyn didn't ask his permission to move her in. She did it on her own. This is what happens when you do that.

"I'm not going to kick her out because she has nowhere else to go. She can't live with my parents 'cause they're too old and won't be able to make sure she goes to school and does her homework. Only thing Mama gonna make sure of is that she goes to church."

"Naw, we not gonna kick her out. I'm just gonna ignore her. After so many times, she'll leave me alone."

"Okay. And I won't say nothing about it. We just gonna move on."

"Fa sho'," Daniel agreed.

Chapter 19

Shelia and James showed up at Rosalyn's and Daniel's house to pick up Michelle after she'd been there for three days. Michelle had missed a day of school, and her parents didn't care. Michelle being gone brought peace to the house.

Robert was just a teenager with raging hormones. He was in the stage of life where he couldn't contain or control himself. Michelle's body was developing, and she loved walking around the house in tank tops and short shorts. I mean, what else was supposed to happen? If Michelle didn't want to be touched by Robert, she should cover up. Her mom tried to tell her that, but children don't listen.

"She still won't tell us what happened," Rosalyn told Shelia.

"You know Michelle is just dramatic. She's at the age where she loves attention. She's starting to really act just like Jasmine acts."

"Yeah," Shelia said, hesitatingly, "I know all about that age. But she was beat up. Badly. When you see her, you'll see her little face is all bruised up and her eye is swollen. We been putting ice on it, but—"

"Rosalyn, when you have kids, you can tell me how to raise mine."

"I said nothing to you about how to raise your children. I was updating you on the status of your child."

"Thank you, Newscaster Rosalyn. Are we expecting rain later?"

"Whatever, Shelia." Rosalyn called Michelle. "Michelle! Your parents are here!"

Michelle went to the living room, head down, too afraid to make eye contact with her parents. What Michelle hadn't told Jasmine was that she told their parents what Robert was doing to her after the first time. Their mom suggested new ways for her to dress to lessen the temptation. Her dad told her that that was to be expected because he was just a boy doing what boys do.

She even told Grams. Grams told her, "Sit down, Baby."

Michelle sat down in the kitchen with Grams while Grams cooked. Michelle was nervous and trembling. She had already told her parents, and they made her feel like it was her fault. What if it was her fault? What if she was wrong for saying something? Jasmine never said anything. Maybe she wasn't supposed to, either.

"Michelle, as girls, young ladies, and women, there are some things we have to endure. It's just the way it is. Lock your door when you sleep. Wear bigger clothes. You know your body is maturing. You're wearing bras now. Maybe you can put on a little weight. You're looking like a model, ya know. And he's noticing.

"And your skin is so light and pretty. Stay outside more so you can get darker. Start spending the night at some friends' houses. Hang out some weekends here with Jasmine. Y'all are so close anyway. If you stay away more and be less attractive, he'll slow down. And maybe even stop. Just pray about it. Ask God to help you to endure. Ask God to make him stop."

"Can't you tell him to stop?"

"Don't sass me."

Michelle sighed. "This happened to you, too, Grams?"

"Oh, Sweetie. I had so many uncles and boy cousins. These things happen."

"How did you get them to stop?"

"I stopped bathing. You could smell my beginnings and endings across the room. That got them to stop. But don't you do that. 'Cause I don't wanna smell that."

"I can't keep going through this, Grams."

"Sing with me: *Like a ship that's tossed and driven battered by an angry sea when the storms of life are raging, and their fury falls on me. I wonder what have I done to make this race so hard to run. Then I say to my soul, 'Don't worry.' The Lord will make a way somehow.*"

Michelle sang the song with her. Grams had her eyes closed, rocking, and waving her hand. Michelle went through the motions of singing a gospel and faking the Holy Ghost moving, but her Spirit was not in it.

Her mom, dad, and grandma told her to tell no one, especially her Paw Paw Wallace. She told Jasmine just to vent. The three days that she spent at Aunt Rosalyn's and Uncle Daniel's allowed her time away to think and see things as clearly as a twelve-year-old could. She made it up in her mind that she wasn't going back home. She wasn't going to be another Jasmine. She would never word it like that to Jasmine, but that's what she concluded.

"Hey, Mom and Dad," Michelle spoke to Shelia and James.

"Let's go home."

Michelle began walking towards the door.

"Hold on, Michelle." Rosalyn grabbed Michelle's shoulder. "What's going on in that house?"

It wasn't clear who she directed the question to, but no one was willing to answer the question anyway. Jasmine walked into the living room.

"Yeah, Mom and Dad. What's going on in that house?" Jasmine asked.

"Two of your daughters are living with us. How much longer until your third daughter is here?" Rosalyn asked Shelia.

"I tell you what, Bitch. None of my daughters gonna be living here. Jasmine, Michelle, come the fuck on."

"No," Rosalyn said. "Y'all can go. We got it from here."

"I will file kidnapping charges on you, Rosalyn. Don't play with me."

"And I will start an investigation into what's going on in your house. Play with me, Trick."

"Rosalyn, just 'cause you can't have kids 'cause you was hot in the ass when you were in college—"

"I was raped! I was not hot in the ass!"

"Hoe, please. All of Southern University know how you was handing that coochie out like pamphlets. Then a nigga burn you, and you wanna holla rape. Girl, stop."

"Say what you want, but these girls are not coming home with you."

"We gonna keep sending you money and stuff for Jasmine since we asked you to take her in. But you on your own with Michelle. Figure it out."

Allowing Michelle to live with her was Rosalyn's way of making it right with Jasmine. She couldn't undo whatever Daniel did to her. She couldn't undo trying to kill her. She wasn't going to undo not addressing certain things. But she could at least take in Jasmine's best friend Michelle and make sure she was safe.

"And for the record," Shelia said to Rosalyn, as she and James were walking out the house, "Denise will never come here and live with y'all. She's the only thing we did right." Shelia looked at Jasmine with a look of disgust. "You caused me to miscarry my last child because of all the shit you put me through. You stressed me the fuck out. All that acting out at school and crying for no damn reason all the time. Had me at the school every damn day.

Putting you through therapy and shit. You get to therapy and don't talk. Had them people looking at us upside our head.

"I wake up and my unborn child is a puddle of blood underneath me. They had to scrape my insides out to get all the baby out. Then that gave me so much damn scarring that I couldn't have no more children. I had to adopt Denise. And she surely was a nice break from your attention-seeking ass. You can rot in this house for all I care. The house became more peaceful when you left, and it's even more peaceful with your sidekick gone. The same bullshit that you pulled, she's starting to pull. Good riddance to the both of you."

James walked out, and Shelia slammed the door behind them.

Rosalyn felt an overwhelming sense of guilt after Shelia said all that to Jasmine. Jasmine was just a child. She didn't deserve that. Rosalyn couldn't take back trying to kill her, but she surely would never to it again. And she internally vowed to take care of Michelle as if she were her own and to protect Michelle from Daniel at all costs.

Chapter 20

"*Your grace and mercy brought me through. I'm living this moment because of you. I wanna thank you and praise you, too. Your grace and mercy brought me through*," Darlene sang, as she was cooking dinner.

"Hey, Grams," Jasmine spoke.

"Hey, Chocolate Pie. I been waiting on you to help me clean all morning. Where you been?"

"Aunt Rosalyn brought me as soon as she woke up. She slept in today."

"Well, you won't believe it, but I'm actually gonna bake a blackberry pie today."

"Really? Why? They're disgusting."

"Watch your mouth. Nothing God creates is disgusting or ugly."

"Well, blackberries are bitter, for sure."

"To each its own. But I love 'em. Especially when I make turnovers."

"Can you add more sugar or something to the pie? That bitterness is strong, Grams."

"Can you just not eat the pie? You act like somebody putting a gun to your head and making you eat it."

"It's just disrespectful to desserts."

Grams and Jasmine laughed.

"You better take God as serious as you take desserts," Grams said.

"I take God more serious, but dessert is like right there underneath."

Jasmine kissed Grams on the cheek. She washed her hands and made the pie crust. While making the pie crust, Grams saw the bruises on Jasmine's neck from the assault by the football players.

"And for the record, Miss Ma'am, blackberries are bitter only when you pluck 'em too early. If you learn some patience, wait a while until they're ready, they'll be the sweetest thing that ever hit your palate," Grams told Jasmine.

"If you say so, Grams."

"*Father, help your children. And don't let them fall by the side of the road. Teach them to love one another. And heaven might find a place in its heart. 'Cause Jesus is love…*," she sang, as she went and found Wallace in the house. She told Wallace that she saw bruises on Jasmine's neck and went back to the kitchen, continuing preparing dinner.

"Black! Come help me pick some blackberries off the fence!"

Jasmine rolled her eyes.

"I told you we were making blackberry pie. I need blackberries," Grams said to Jasmine.

"All the blackberries we pick, I thought you already had some."

"I have *some*, not enough. Go help Wallace get some more berries for this pie."

"I don't even like the pie!"

"Don't sass me, Girl! What has gotten into you today?"

"Jasmine! Outside. Now." Wallace had never taken that tone with her.

Jasmine knew she had messed up. It's just that all of life's weights and pressure had come down on her. She was hiding the rape from her dad, her Uncle Daniel, the football players. Her Aunt Rosalyn possibly tried to kill her and was acting funny with her. Her mom hadn't checked on her at all since dropping her off to Aunt Rosalyn's and Uncle Daniel's eight months ago. Her seventeenth birthday was last week, and nobody said or did anything for it, except her maternal grandparents.

She had sex with John a few days after the football players assaulted her because she felt that was the only way to keep John. She didn't want to have sex at all, but she was worried that he secretly believed his teammates about her being a whore and messing around on him. She wanted to show him that she was his and his only. And she also ruined his eighteenth birthday, so having sex with him was her way of apologizing and giving him a birthday gift. The weight of the sin of fornication was a lot to bear.

She had forced her baby sister Michelle to keep quiet about their dad raping her; in turn, she had to keep quiet about Robert raping Michelle. Jasmine just wanted to get in her zone and let her mind breathe. But she got to her grandparents', and her granddaddy hollered about picking some got damn blackberries off the got damn fence. She just wanted to cook. That's how she de-stressed. She loved Paw Paw Wallace, but shit! Give her a break before she breaks!

"I'm sorry, Grams," Jasmine said, as she walked outside to pick the got damn blackberries off the got damn fence.

"Who pissed in your Wheaties, Blackberry?" Wallace asked her.

"The whole world," she answered, as they picked blackberries.

"Talk to me about it. Who is the world?"

Jasmine sighed. "Nobody, Paw Paw. I just wanted a day not doing this."

"Who is the world? And did the world put those marks on your neck?"

Jasmine grabbed her neck and gasped. She had forgotten all about those marks. She didn't cover them up with make-up that day.

She couldn't pretend like everything was fine anymore. She laid on Wallace's chest and sobbed. She could feel his breathing pattern change and breaths get deeper. He stroked her hair and tried to speak as calmly as possible.

"Tell me who did this. I can make that person disappear like magic."

"Some boys at school took turns on me, Paw Paw."

"Who?" he asked, attempting to remain calm.

"I don't know. They snuck up behind me, pinned me down, and bent me over. I never saw anyone. But I think it was five of them."

"Did any voice sound familiar?"

"Not at all. I'm not even sure they went to the school. May not have even been students at all. I just don't know."

Jasmine didn't want to get anyone in trouble. She didn't want all that attention. And she didn't want John to know about the true character of his "friends". She just needed to vent. That's it.

"Chocolate Baby Doll, you gotta tell the truth. That's the only way we can make this right."

"I don't need it made right. I just need it to had never happened." The tears started up again.

Wallace continued to console and embrace Jasmine. "When you're ready to tell the truth and let justice be served, I'll be here, okay?"

Jasmine nodded her head while lying on his chest.

"Paw Paw got your back."

"I know."

"I won't tell nobody. This is between me and you. We don't need this getting out if you ain't gonna let me do anything about it. But as soon as you give me a name, I'm making the news. You hear me?"

"Yes, Sir."

"You did nothing to deserve this. They were some demons who will pay. You better believe that. I told you dead bodies make great fertilizer. They gone make us some money. But whenever you're ready."

Wallace tried his hardest to maintain his composure in front of Jasmine. He knew if he blew up and exploded and caused a scene, she would never open up and say anything to him. But behind closed doors and internally, he was in a rage. Some niggas were dumb enough to mess with his granddaughter. Whether she admitted who it was or not, Wallace would make them pay for their sins, or he would die trying.

Chapter 21

"You didn't call that boy all weekend," Aunt Rosalyn said to Jasmine, as Jasmine walked into the house. "I started to give him Mama and Daddy number so he could call you while you were at they house this weekend. Girl, what's wrong with you?"

"I just didn't feel like talking."

"You didn't feel like talking?! I saw that li'l boy's stats. He's gonna make it on somebody's professional football team. Maybe even the New Orleans Saints. But you over here 'don't feel like talking'."

"Well, I don't. If he makes it big, good for him."

Jasmine tried not to disappear on him again like he asked her not to. But talking to Paw Paw Wallace stirred up all kinds of emotions and thoughts. She just didn't want to be around John or have anything to do with him after what his "friends" did to her.

Part of her was bitter that he wasn't around that morning to protect her. She knew it was his birthday, and his coach took him out to eat for a birthday breakfast, but still. He wasn't there for her. A piece of her felt that he was lingering in the background watching as she was passed and tossed around. She knew it wasn't true, but her paranoia and anger had her feeling all types of ways.

Deep down inside she knew that he was innocent and ignorant to all that had taken place. She just needed something to project her feelings onto. Her feelings of inadequacy were becoming heavier and heavier as the days went by.

Like Aunt Rosalyn said, he was definitely going to make it big on somebody's professional football team. What would she look like on his arm? She was garbage, trash, filth, raggedy, damaged. She had no business being with him.

She decided to just let him be great without her. He didn't need the weight and baggage that she brought. It was almost the end of the school year anyway. In a few months, they'd graduate, enjoy their summer, go to different colleges, and forget that they ever were a thing.

"What is all this about, Jasmine? Talk to me," Aunt Rosalyn said.

Jasmine wasn't sure if she could talk to her or not. She knew not to trust anything that came out of Uncle Daniel's mouth, but him saying that Rosalyn tried to kill her constantly played in her mind. She was careful around Aunt Rosalyn. She never let her guard down with her.

"I just want to focus on school," Jasmine said. "He's distracting me."

Rosalyn remembered how she felt after she was sexually assaulted. She withdrew from everyone, especially the ones who loved her the most. It was as if she felt she didn't deserve anyone's love. She knew that Jasmine was the poster child for sexual assault victims. If Daniel didn't have that leverage on Rosalyn, she would have handled the situation a lot differently. She would have had his ass thrown in jail for rape. But he tied her hands. She just had to watch, observe, and know in silence.

Chapter 22

Three weeks had gone by since Jasmine told Paw Paw Wallace about the assault. She was avoiding John at school at all costs. He wouldn't let up, though. He wanted her. He felt that God told him she was the one. If he could just crack her code, they would get back together.

Jasmine missed John so badly that it hurt. He was never not on her mind. Whether she was thinking about his smile or worried that he had another girl, John occupied Jasmine's brain.

He had no other girl, though. Jasmine was all he could think about. He racked his brain wondering what did he do wrong? Did he not make her feel loved enough? Was he too busy with football? Were his siblings too loud whenever he was on the phone with Jasmine? What?

Rosalyn observed Jasmine. She knew exactly what was wrong with her and why she was all of a sudden to herself and avoiding John. John still called every day, hoping to get to talk to Jasmine.

Rosalyn wanted to comfort Jasmine. She was not sold on the "your niece is fast" story Daniel gave her. Even if Jasmine was "fast", Daniel had no right to touch her.

Rosalyn had been raped in college. She knew the feelings of loneliness, confusion, depression, disgust, etcetera. She knew that Jasmine was going through this by herself, and that was not safe. She remembered all the thoughts that she had and all the things she did trying to cope.

Jasmine was in a dangerous place mentally by Rosalyn's assumptions. It was time for her to be an aunt. She had forgiven herself for trying to kill Jasmine. It was a fly by night feeling she had. She felt guilty every second of the day for trying to kill her. She couldn't stomach the facts about what she did.

She was so grateful to God that her plan didn't work. She would never try that again. Ever. She had grown to love and adore Jasmine. She missed her whenever she was away. She wasn't sure if Jasmine knew that she intentionally put shrimp in her grits. If she did know, she never addressed her about it. She didn't know how to approach Jasmine about anything, but she would figure it out.

Little did she know, Daniel was the least of Jasmine's worries. Jasmine's period was five weeks late, she was throwing up all the time, and her appetite was unprecedented. At first, Jasmine thought it was the stress of it all. But as the days went by, and her symptoms increased and worsened, it didn't take a rocket scientist or a genius to know what was going on. She was pregnant.

To make matters worse, she had no idea who the father was. There was no chance it was Daniel because he hadn't assaulted her in months. She hadn't had sex with E in months. Her dad hadn't assaulted her in almost a year. It was a toss-up between the five football players and John.

Jasmine told no one. Abortion was not an option at all. God would be so mad at her. It didn't matter to her that she was raped, causing a pregnancy. It was still a life that God allowed. God would not justify that murder.

She decided she would pray the baby away. If praying didn't work, she would suck in her stomach the entire pregnancy. If she couldn't suck in her stomach, she would wear bigger clothes. The problem with that was that she didn't have money to buy a pickle from the candy lady, let alone buy a new wardrobe.

Ah-ha! Lightbulb moment. She would get a job. The more she stayed away, the less her family would see her. That decreased the chances of them seeing her and knowing she was pregnant. That would also give her income to be able to buy her new wardrobe.

She had it all figured out. If she couldn't pray the baby away, and she had to have the baby, she would hide the pregnancy the whole time. Whenever she would go in labor, she'd run to the bathroom, have the baby, walk out the bathroom with a baby, and say, "Look what I found in the bathroom." Her family would turn the baby in to a fire station or something like that. She would never admit to the baby being hers. She would claim that a random baby popped up in the bathroom. That was her story, and she was sticking to it.

Then she thought about what if she went in labor at a store or at work or at school. Well, that would be perfect. She would have the baby in the bathroom and walk out like nothing happened. She'd pray that her baby ended up in the hands of a good family, and life would be great for everyone.

Sigh. The only problem with all of her plans was that they all included her having no part of her child's life. The more time went by, the more she realized that she couldn't do that. She just couldn't.

She couldn't just drop a baby off in a bathroom and act like nothing happened. She couldn't just walk away from her flesh and blood. That would make her no better than all the men who leave their kids with their mothers and act like they never had any children. She would be contributing to the parentless children epidemic that was overtaking Louisiana.

She realized that she was trying to handle this pregnancy as if it were a *thing* or a task or something to scratch off her to-do list. But this was a baby. A child. A life. Her baby. Her child. A life that she created.

No, the situation was not ideal. If the baby wasn't John's, the situation was not even her choice. But once all the smoke cleared, the fact would still remain that this was God's child first and hers second. She would not make a child pay for someone else's mistakes. Her grandma would always say that God will give you beauty for ashes.

Her assault was the ashes; the baby would be the beauty.

She decided to keep the baby. And when the baby got older, she would tell the baby how he or she was a blessing in the midst of mess. How he or she was the testimony from the test.

Whether a boy or girl, she would name the baby Journey. Journey meant daylight. Jasmine's favorite scripture was Jeremiah 29:11, "For I know the thoughts that I think toward you, saith the Lord, thoughts of peace, and not evil, to give you an expected end." That scripture always meant a new beginning to her, a new day—daylight.

Chapter 23

Oddly enough, as much as Jasmine hated blackberries and hated picking them off the fence, she loved picking them off the fence with her baby sister Denise. Maybe she hated picking them so much with her granddad because it was always as if he had a hidden agenda. He always needed her to talk. He was always trying to pry information out of her.

But with Denise, there was no pressure at all. Denise didn't care if Jasmine talked or not. Denise's imagination never cut off, which meant that her mouth never shut up. She did all the talking for her and Jasmine. And as long as she had Jasmine to herself, she was on top of the world.

Jasmine was a victim of her dad, and Michelle was a victim of their brother. James said he would never touch Michelle or Denise because of their beautiful light skin, but obviously, Robert didn't care about that. Jasmine had to make sure that Denise wasn't a victim of Robert or anybody else. She just didn't know how to ask a six-year-old.

As Jasmine and Denise picked blackberries off the fence, Jasmine's mind was a tornado thinking how she could word her concerns without confusing Denise or setting off alarms.

Denise continued in her conversation that Jasmine had stopped listening to a long time ago. "…and then my parrot flew to the neighbor's house and told them that their couch was ugly. The girl neighbor choked the parrot. The parrot— I named the parrot Aladdin— the parrot flew back to my room through the vent and told me the girl neighbor choked him. So, I walked to the girl neighbor and asked her, 'Did you choke Aladdin?' And I was so shocked at what she said."

"What did she say, Denise?"

"She said, 'Yes, I choked that ugly bird.' She didn't even lie about it!"

Did Denise have a parrot? No. She probably never even saw one in real life. She didn't even have a girl neighbor. All their neighbors were damn near retirement age. But these things were real in Denise's six-year-old mind, so Jasmine just let her be. She allowed her to be a kid as long as life would allow it.

"So, what did you do about the girl neighbor choking Aladdin?" Jasmine asked her.

"I choked the girl neighbor," Denise answered.

Jasmine had to stop picking the blackberries off the fence to laugh.

"What did her mama do about you choking her daughter?"

"Nothing because she was scared that I would choke her, too."

"Okay," Jasmine said, sarcastically.

"So now the girl neighbor and her mama don't talk to me no more. The girl neighbor's mama said that me and her daughter can't play together no more. And I don't care because I don't want to play with nobody who chokes birds. Birds arc people, too."

"You are absolutely correct, Denise."

"And then the girl neighbor's dad…"

Denise's stories had no end. You had to just cut her off or ignore her. Usually, the latter happened. She would ramble on and on to where your mind would drift, and whenever you came to, she'd still be talking.

"Is anybody touching you between your legs?" Jasmine asked Denise, cutting off her story.

"Mama do every day when she bathe me."

"Anybody else?"

"Sometimes Grams if she has to bathe me."

"Anybody else?"

"My parrot when he bathes me."

Jasmine huffed and rolled her eyes.

"Anybody putting anything between your legs besides soap, water, and a towel?"

"No. Why would they? What I do wrong?" Denise asked, in a panic.

"Nothing! You did everything right. I just want to make sure you're safe. If someone touches you between your legs, and they're not cleaning you, you tell me, okay? Even if they tell you not to tell me. Okay?"

"Okay. So Aladdin got a haircut and drove to work…"

Chapter 24

Jasmine's cycle was now ten weeks late. She wasn't showing, and she had no concern about showing any time soon. She was a chubby girl with a pudgy stomach. No one would notice. Plus, it was winter, so she wore hoodies all day, and no one thought of anything of it.

Jasmine was still avoiding John at all costs. She had no intention of telling him she was pregnant. She was going to let him enjoy his life without having anything to do with her. She felt that she owed him that much.

"Don't act like you don't see me," John said to Jasmine in their high school's hallway. "I gotta ask you something."

Usually, Jasmine would keep walking. But this day, it was as if something told her to stop and listen. "Wassup?"

"Why haven't your face broke out?" he asked her.

She thought about that question and was confused. "Huh?"

"Every month around your period, your face breaks out bad. Especially your chin and forehead. Your skin been clear. Why?"

Jasmine's breath left her body. She had no idea he paid that much attention to her. "I been drinking more water," she answered.

He leaned into her and quietly asked, "Are you pregnant, Jasmine? Is that why you've been avoiding me?"

"I began avoiding you before I found out I was pregnant."

Before she realized it, she had admitted to being pregnant. His eyes glowed up, and a smile spread across his face. "I'm here, Jasmine. I ain't going nowhere. I'll quit the football team and get three jobs if I have to. I'm here. I swear."

The bell rang. It was time for the next class.

"We'll talk at lunch, okay?"

"Okay," she agreed.

She hated social studies class. That class period always seemed to drag along. But this day, it seemed as if the class was over as soon as she sat down. She was not looking forward to talking to John, but he wasn't going to let it go.

"First things first, how are you?" John asked Jasmine at lunch. They were sitting outside, away from anyone's earshot.

"Journey had me nauseated in the beginning. I'm good now. I drink ginger ale before I get up. That helps a lot."

"That's good to know, but I'm asking how are you, outside of—you named the baby already? Journey? I like that. But how are you doing outside of Journey? I haven't talked to you in so long."

"Oh, I'm fine. What about you? I see you got a little chubby since football season is over with. You wanna be me so bad," Jasmine joked.

"Naw. You had me stressin'. I ate my way through. But you know I'mma be here for Journey. Especially after my parents made my ex best friend abort her baby when I was fourteen. I'm eighteen now. They can't make me or you do shit we don't wanna do. I'mma be a daddy for real this time."

Jasmine looked at him in his eyes as he spoke. He meant every word. She wouldn't deny him the opportunity to be a great father. She just couldn't be with him.

"And I'mma be a great husband, too. We'll get married as soon as you turn eighteen. We'll be a big, happy family. White picket fence. A dog. And a Black president."

Jasmine chuckled. "I want a pink fence instead of a white one. I rather a cat. And America will never vote for a Black president. But I ain't here to crush your dreams."

"So, you'll marry me?"

"No, John. I don't want to be with you. I'm sorry I wasted your time. But you're going to be a great father to Journey."

"Why don't you want me? What did I do?"

"I just want to be alone. Don't push the issue. Please."

John was quiet for a moment. "Is Journey a girl or a boy?"

"I don't know."

"When do you find out?"

"I've never been to the doctor. I don't know."

"What you mean you never been to the doctor?"

"I been hiding my pregnancy. So, I can't go to no doctor. And Aunt Rosalyn and Uncle Daniel got my insurance card. I can't take my own self to the doctor because I'm still a minor. I think. I really don't even know. But in order for me to find out, I'd have to ask for my insurance card. And they're gonna ask why I want it. I just don't wanna go through all that. I ain't answering no questions, and I ain't going to no doctor."

"No. We gotta take care of Journey. I'll be by your house today and talk to your aunt and uncle. You gotta go to the doctor."

Jasmine had never seen that look on his face before nor heard that tone of voice before coming from him. She knew he was serious. She didn't want to test him, but dammit, she was scared. Up until a few seconds ago, she had no intention of telling him. This entire time, her plan had been to hide the pregnancy until further notice. And in the blink of an eye, those plans went to him and the whole world knowing.

"I need a second to get my thoughts together, John."

"If you were three weeks pregnant, I'd accept that. But you're not. Your face haven't broke out in a minute. How far along are you?"

"I'm ten weeks late."

"Yeah. You gotta go to the doctor. Your people gotta know. Give me your address. I'm coming today to talk to them."

"And what about your parents?" Jasmine asked John.

"I'll tell them as soon as I get home."

"How are they gonna react?" Jasmine asked, nervously.

"I don't know. And it don't even matter. What they ain't gone do is make you kill our baby. See you tonight."

John pecked her on the cheek. Lunch was over. They went to their classes.

She wondered should she tell her aunt and uncle that John was coming by. Should she tell them why he was coming by? Should she cushion the blow? Should she prepare them? Should she let them be blindsided? What was the proper course of action to take?

Knock, knock, knock.

Jasmine's stomach dropped to her toes. She had never been so nervous in her life. She decided to let them be blindsided.

"Who the hell is that?" Uncle Daniel asked.

Of all days for them both to be at home...

Aunt Rosalyn looked out the window. "Ohhh," she sung, "Jasmine's *boyfriend* is here. I was wondering when you would have him over."

Aunt Rosalyn let him in. Jasmine couldn't pretend to be happy to see him to save her life. She loved him and hated him at the same time for doing this.

"Mrs. Rougeau, how are you? I'm John."

"Baby, I know who you are. Come on in. Jasmine, don't be rude. Greet your man. Fix him some water. Do something!"

Jasmine happily ran to the kitchen to get him a glass of water. She needed just a few more seconds to herself.

"Mr. Rougeau. Hello." John extended his hand for Daniel to shake. "How you doing?"

Who this li'l nigga is, looking me in my eyes when he talk to me? He ain't no grown man, Daniel thought to himself. He shook his hand. "I'm good. How you?"

"Doing well, Sir."

"Have a seat, John. Me and Daniel will give you and Jasmine your space."

"Actually, I came here to talk to y'all."

Jasmine walked in when John told them that he wanted to talk to them. She turned right back around and went back to the kitchen. She began hyperventilating. All three of them walked into the kitchen to talk when they noticed Jasmine going through it.

"Did you have seafood?!" Aunt Rosalyn asked her.

Jasmine shook her head no and began breathing into a paper bag.

"Jasmine, I'm here. You're not going through this alone." John held her hand and removed the paper bag from her mouth. "Come sit down."

Jasmine's breathing eased up, and she sat down at the kitchen table. Uncle Daniel and Aunt Rosalyn were on one side, and Jasmine and Daniel were on the other side of the table.

"Jasmine is pregnant," John said.

Jasmine could have sworn she saw stars when he said that.

John continued, "About two and a half to three months, we assume. She has not gone to a doctor to get checked because she was trying to hide it, I guess. I don't know. But she has to go to the doctor. So, can y'all give her, her insurance card so she can go to the doctor?"

"Wait a minute." Aunt Rosalyn held her hand up and sighed. "What?"

"Jasmine is pregnant," John repeated.

"By who?!" Aunt Rosalyn asked.

"By me."

"Boy, you stupider than you look. Did Jasmine tell you how she fucked my husband, and she has another boyfriend who is a grown ass man that people see her riding around town with named E?"

Jasmine's face dropped.

"You thought I didn't know about E? You thought I didn't know about you wanting my husband? Wanting to be me? Wanting to take my place?"

"Your husband raped me repeatedly with a loaded gun in my mouth when I was sixteen and seventeen up until a few months ago! I was a victim!"

"Bitch, you was about as much as victim as Carolyn Bryant was when she accused Emmett Till of sexually harassing her. You persuaded him, enticed him—"

Now it all made sense to John. Why she hesitated when asked if she was a virgin. Why she would come and go. Why she wouldn't let him call her for fear of her uncle being home. He knew that she had been raped.

"Your husband is a grown ass man. And you knew that they had done something? And you did nothing about it? But you want to accuse her of doing something to *your* husband? A *child* at the time?"

"Boy, you a grown ass man yourself. Don't think you can't go to jail just because y'all are both seniors in high school. You are still eighteen, and she is still a kid. Anyway, while you worried about who preyed on who, you need to worry about if you the daddy or not."

John was worried about that, but it wasn't the time to let that be known. It also never occurred to him that he had committed statutory rape. They had been classmates since ninth grade. In no type of way did he prey on her or entice her or anything like that. He fell in love with her when he was a kid. He just happened to turn eighteen a few months before she did. It wasn't criminal behavior; it was just semantics.

"My concern is Jasmine, as yours should be."

Jasmine was Rosalyn's concern until she found out Jasmine was pregnant. The hate that she used to have for Jasmine came rushing back with a mighty roar. How the hell could Jasmine sit up in her house and do something for her husband that she couldn't do—have his baby?! The audacity!

"And where this baby supposed to stay? Jasmine ain't got no job," Rosalyn said to John.

"I can get a job!" Jasmine quickly said.

"And where the baby gone live?"

Jasmine and John were both silent. Truthfully, they both were banking on Journey living with Jasmine in Aunt Rosalyn's and Uncle Daniel's house.

"John, you have no house for her to live in. You live with your parents. Little Boy, being eighteen is nothing but a number when you have *nothing* to offer anybody. You are not daddy material. You are still a child with an adult's age," Rosalyn said.

Daniel sat at the table and said absolutely nothing. He was ecstatic about the thought of being a daddy. He contained the smile on his face, but he couldn't contain the smile in his heart.

"First and foremost, there is no chance of Uncle Daniel being the father. He hasn't raped me in about four months."

Daniel's heart was crushed.

"What about E and God knows who else you done opened your legs to?"

"Are you taking her to the doctor or not?" John asked Aunt Rosalyn.

"Not," she answered.

"Wow. But you grown, though."

"As a matter of fact, I'm so grown that she gotta get the hell up out my house. Let her mama and daddy take her and their grandchild to the doctor."

"She left their house for a reason," John said.

" 'Cause she a damn problem."

"Hi," Michelle said, walking in the kitchen, looking around confused. "What's going on?"

"I'm getting kicked out," Jasmine told Michelle.

"Ya damn right." Rosalyn called Shelia on the phone. "Your damn fast ass daughter is pregnant. She can't stay here no more. That Black ass whore of a niece is causing too many fucking problems. I tried to with her, but I can't. Get your child and your grandchild. That's right. Your grandchild. She been fucking my husband. Fucking him so good that he didn't even want me. She claims this baby ain't his. But that bitch lies so much, who knows? Hell. She probably don't know who the daddy is."

Jasmine went to her room and began packing her belongings. John followed her and helped her.

"I will take you to your parents' house," he said.

Jasmine didn't want to go there. She would rather have been homeless. If Journey wasn't in her belly, she would have chosen a cardboard box on the side of the road.

"Thank you," Jasmine said.

"I'm coming with you," Michelle said.

"No. You stay here. And you know why," Jasmine told her.

"No. We're in this together. Forever," Michelle rebutted.

"No. Not in this. Stay here where you're safe."

"I'm only safe here because you're here. As soon as you leave, I won't be safe anymore. I might as well come with you."

John listened without letting it be known that he was listening. *Why isn't home safe? Should I even be taking them there?* he thought to himself.

John, Michelle, and Jasmine loaded up in John's car and left. Tears streamed down Jasmine's face the entire car ride. John went back and forth between holding her hand and holding Michelle's hand.

"I'm John by the way," he said to Michelle.

"That's an old name."

"I was named after my great granddad."

"Why?"

"My dad loved his granddad."

"I love my granddad, too, but no child deserves to be named Wallace. No matter how terrible they are," Michelle said.

That made Jasmine's tears stop for a few seconds and allow a smile to appear on her face. Truth be told, her granddad could have been named Timbuktu, and she wouldn't mind naming her child that. She understood John's dad loving his granddad so much that he would name a child after him. If Journey didn't have such a powerful meaning behind it, she would name her child Wallace, too—boy or girl. Who cares?

"Wallace ain't a bad name. I mean, he could be named Willie Earl. Or Henry. Or Jethro," John said.

"Jethro?! Who in the world named their child Jethro? How you even spell that?"

"My Uncle Jethro is a great man," he said.

"He better be. With that name, nothing else better be wrong with him. His name used up all the amount of wrongs he is allowed in his lifetime."

John laughed so hard that he forgot all that had transpired that night. It was his first time meeting Michelle, and she left an impression on him that he'd never forget.

His mind did wander and think about other boys possibly being Journey's dad. It had never crossed his mind that he wasn't the only option. Was E someone she was having sex with? Could he possibly be the dad? Are there others? How many?

But he loved her so much that he didn't want to know. As long as she never told him that he may not be the daddy, he wouldn't push the issue. Even if it wasn't his baby, he would treat Journey as if he or she was anyway. It was his opportunity to make it right from the abortion his ex best friend was forced to get years ago.

He dropped Jasmine and Michelle off at their parents'. Jasmine stopped him from going into the house. She thanked him for being there and for all that he had done. She told him that it just wasn't the best time to meet her parents. She knew them. She needed time alone with them first.

"I never meant for all this to happen. I am so sorry," he said.

"All this stuff had been swept under the rug. It was bound to come out anyway. You did nothing wrong. See you at school tomorrow."

"See you at school tomorrow. And we done been through too much at this point for you to act like you don't see me at school."

Jasmine smirked. "I'll wave at you tomorrow."

"I got your wave. I can show you better than I can tell you."

They both laughed.

"And I will find somewhere for us to stay. My word is bond," John promised.

Jasmine and Michelle got their things out of the car and walked into the house.

Here we go...

Chapter 25

John looked for Jasmine all day at school. He searched the city bus stops, school bus stops, car rider lanes, car driver lanes, and walkers' lanes. No sight of Jasmine anywhere. She wasn't in their biology class, either.

"Your game is off, John. Glad it's just practice cuz yo' head is nowhere near in the game," his football coach told him. "Tighten up!"

John tried to "tighten up", but he couldn't. Too much was on his mind.

"Wassup with you, Bruh? Talk to me," Damien said to John after practice. "I ain't never seen you this bad."

John hadn't told Damien about Jasmine being pregnant because Damien always had something negative to say about her. Yeah, Damien and John were best friends, but when it came down to Jasmine, conversation was off limits.

"I'm good. See you tomorrow."

"Naw. I know when something on your mind. Let it off."

John exhaled. He made sure no one was around to hear what they were talking about. "Jasmine is pregnant."

Damien's eyes got big at the thought of the baby being his. "How far along is she?"

"We guess three months."

Fuck! Damien thought to himself.

"And we told her aunt and uncle last night. They kicked her out, sent her back to her parents', and I ain't heard from her since. I just hope she's okay. I put her in that situation. And I ain't even got nowhere for her to stay."

"Don't trip it. It probably ain't even your baby," Damien said.

"Why the fuck would you say that? That's why I didn't say shit to you in the first place."

"Cuz, we call Jasmine 'Air'. She's for everybody."

"Say that shit again, My Nigga."

John walked up to Damien, chest to chest. Damien backed up. Damien had no proof that Jasmine was sleeping with anybody other than John. He was jealous of how happy she made John; he was jealous that she didn't want him. He was mad that despite him always telling John to leave her, he didn't. John always listened to Damien. John always did what Damien told him to do. Now, he had his own mind, and Damien didn't like that. All these problems started with Jasmine. She had to go.

"I'm not trying to fall out with you behind no bitch."

John swung on him, connected to Damien's chin, and he never stopped hitting him. Even when Damien was on the ground, John never let up. Damien picked the wrong day. In addition to Jasmine being M.I.A., he didn't have a number to call her. He had Aunt Rosalyn's and Uncle Daniel's number; he didn't have her parents' number. In addition to that, when he told his parents, they told him that they would have nothing to do with Journey. They said Journey could never come to their house. That Journey was the representation of him destroying his life.

"You just can't control your dick, can you? We saved your career the first time; we ain't saving it again," his dad told him.

And in the back of John's mind, he wondered if Journey was his. He trusted Jasmine. If there was a chance that Journey wasn't his, Jasmine would tell him, right? But who was E?

All of John's questions, frustrations, sadness, anger were taken out on Damien's face.

There was no chance of the baby being E's. The timing was off. But there was a chance that it was one of the five football players'.

The coach saw John brutally attacking Damien and pulled him off of him. "This is between y'all. Y'all are two grown men. I'mma stay out of it. But I couldn't sit back and watch you kill him," he said to John.

The camera that Damien always carried around ended on the ground after their scuffle. John stomped the camera into pieces, hurting Damien more. John walked away with Damien's blood on his fists and pieces of Damien's camera on the bottom of his shoe.

Chapter 26

Things went better at her parents' house than Jasmine thought. Her mama told her, "Took you longer than I thought to get pregnant." Shelia said nothing else to her. Denise was so excited to see her back home. She had seen her almost every weekend at their grandparents' house, but there was no place like home.

When Jasmine saw Robert, she told him that his days of touching Michelle were over. He asked her, "And what you gonna do about it? You barely do anything about James touching you."

"If you wanna find out, go ahead," Jasmine told Robert.

Robert was so furious that Jasmine was back that he tore up the house. He threw things, punched holes in the walls, yelled, screamed, and ripped pillows apart. "We were better without her!" he yelled.

Her daddy was waiting on her to come back home because he was missing her. Not missing her the way a dad misses his daughter… he satisfied his missing her that night. He told her, "You can't get pregnant. Why not?" Jasmine didn't fight it at all. She wanted to keep her baby as safe as possible.

But in her mind, things would go so much worse once she made it home. She thanked God that it didn't. But she knew that she couldn't stay there. That was no place for Journey. She began mentally planning her exit. She knew she had to be honest with John about everything, even if that meant that he wouldn't get her and Journey a place to live. She wasn't going to enter the chapter of motherhood with lies and secrets.

Chapter 27

Jasmine decided that she wasn't going to miss another day of school. She'd missed one day of school, and that was enough. It hurt her to her soul that she missed one day of school. She had perfect attendance ever since she was in second grade. She messed that up and couldn't get it back. She beat herself up for it, but she wasn't going to miss two days. She had plans of being a veterinarian, and no Uncle Daniel, Dad, Damien, or football players were going to change that. She decided to put her emotions in check and get her head back in the game.

She realized that the devil sent so much to destroy her and to knock her off course. He really put his all into attacking her hands through multiple rapes, trying to make it impossible for her to become a veterinarian. He knew that if he could destroy her hands, she couldn't become a veterinarian, that would kill her dreams, and killed dreams would kill her. But he wasn't going to win. Jasmine made sure of that.

When she got off the school bus, a student who she'd only seen in passing, but didn't know, put a balled up paper in her hand. When Jasmine unballed the paper, it read **Stay away from John and go find your real baby daddy. Better yet, kill it and kill yourself.**

It didn't take a rocket scientist to know that it was from Damien. Damien sent a flunky girl who he was stringing along to pass the message to Jasmine. Jasmine threw the note in the trash and continued walking to her class. She noticed everyone was staring at her and whispering.

Am I being paranoid? People don't even know me. No one barely talks to me at school. I don't even have friends here. No way people know. John is the only one who knows. He wouldn't have told anyone without telling me. Without asking me. I'm just paranoid.

She sat down at her desk in first period. Her classmates were looking at her there, too. About seven minutes into class, someone threw a piece of paper at her and fake coughed, "Whore."

She kept a face of steel. No one could read her, but she was in shambles internally. Why would John do this to her? What did she do to him to make him turn on her so quickly? She never even requested that he be a father, so he could have just moved on with his life like he never knew about Journey.

Why?!

"Do you need help getting out of your seat?" a female classmate asked her once class was over. "Don't want you bumping that stomach on your way up."

The entire class laughed and walked out the classroom. She swallowed her emotions and got up.

"I'm going to let your parents know that you are in no condition to be at this school. It's not safe," her teacher said, then walked away.

Jasmine walked to the bathroom, locked herself in a stall, and cried. When she heard someone come into the bathroom, she sucked her tears up. She'd be damned if someone knew they had hit her where it hurt. She got herself together quickly and walked out with her head held high.

"John finna be the next Deion Sanders. Leave him alone. You wasn't nothing but a pity fuck anyway," a female classmate told her as she walked into biology.

John had been getting harassed all day, too. From girls telling him he deserved better than Jasmine to dudes telling him not to let that "burnt piece of toast" ruin his career. He told everyone who approached him that he was in love with her and to get the fuck out his face.

He wasn't worried about what people were saying to him; he was worried about what people were saying to her. And it all stemmed from him telling Damien. He didn't know Damien would do this. He thought they'd discuss it and it'd stay between them. This was worse than he could've ever imagined. He would **never** put Jasmine in that type of predicament.

He purposely sat in the seat next to Jasmine's in biology class. They had assigned seats, but he didn't care. He needed her to see him, see him.

When she walked in and saw him sitting in the seat next to her, she walked out of the classroom. She had said that morning that emotions were no longer going to control her life, but this took her off guard. This was too much for her.

"Jasmine!" John ran behind her. "I need to talk to you. I did *not* do this!"

This time, Jasmine didn't care who was watching. She was crying, face full of tears, shoulders shaking. "You're the only one who knew. Why did you do this to me? I've been getting threatening notes from Damien all day telling me to get an abortion and to leave you alone. You did this! I confided in you when I didn't even want to!"

"I told Damien because I thought he was my best friend. He told everybody and twisted the story. I love you. I have since the eleventh grade. I would never hurt you. Please believe me."

Emotions were too high. She wanted to believe him, but it was too soon in her feelings to make that decision. She believed that John would never do this to her or anybody, but she just didn't know. She also knew how much of a snake Damien was. This was definitely not beneath him.

"I love you, Jasmine. I mean that shit. I got us. I spent all day yesterday looking for an apartment for us and Journey. And I got us one. We move in in ten days. I'm for real about you. About us. And when I say us, I mean Journey, too."

"You really got somewhere for us to live?"

"Yes. I need y'all safe. And I could tell that your parents' house ain't it."

"Do y'all have a hall pass?" a teacher asked them.

"No, Ma'am," they answered in unison.

"Then get to class."

Jasmine turned to head to class. John stopped her.

"What?" she asked him.

He held his hand out for her to grab. She grabbed it. They walked into biology class holding hands for the world to see. John was serious about her, and nobody was going to change his mind.

Chapter 28

"We got a call from the principal of your school. You had a hell of a day today, huh?" Jasmine's mom asked her.

"Yeah, I did."

"Your principal thinks it's best that you go to a different school. You've caused quite an uproar in them people's hallway. I think it's best that you go to a different school and move out. You ain't been acting right here. You just cause problems everywhere you go."

"I will not change schools. I'm finna be graduating in a few months. I ain't hurting nobody by being pregnant. They are choosing to be evil towards me. I ain't did nothing to nobody. I'mma walk across that stage, and they ain't gotta worry about me ever again. I refuse to leave my school. But I will leave this house."

Once again, Jasmine was gathering up the little bit of belongings that she had to move away. She fit all the clothes and books that she could in three backpacks and caught the city bus to her grandparents' house. She hated leaving Denise and Michelle again, but it had to be done.

Ten days was a short time, but when waiting on something, that is forever. In ten days, she could move into the place John had for her and Journey. She didn't know if he would move in, too. He probably told her if he would or not, but that day had been filled with so many emotions, she didn't remember those details.

The entire bus ride, she looked at her right hand. The hand he purposefully, loudly, proudly, boldly held as they walked into biology class. She hated to be like a ten-year-old girl, but she thought to herself that she'd never wash that hand again. That gesture meant so much to her that she felt like her right hand was a prize that she had to guard with her life.

"Can I move in for ten days?" Jasmine asked Grams as soon as Grams opened the door.

Grams looked at her and said, "Why just ten days? That baby gonna need somewhere to stay, and under a bridge ain't gone cut it."

"Who told you? Mama? Dad? Uncle Daniel? Aunt Rosalyn?"

"God."

"God?" Jasmine asked.

"God," Grams repeated. "Come on in. Put your stuff in that back room you been thinking is yours since you been four years old. Once you get settled, dinner will be ready. We'll sup and talk."

Jasmine settled in, did homework, and showered. Once she had done all that, dinner was ready as Grams promised.

"This is delicious as always, Grams."

"Thank you. Wallace working late tonight. Every time it rains, he be late getting home."

"Well, he drives them big ole trucks. He gotta slow down before he kills somebody, including himself. So, yes, he gonna be late, Grams."

"You right. I just worry every time that he's late because something happened. They won't let the drivers put those car phones in their trucks. Sometimes, he can call me from a store. But usually when it's raining this bad, he's not getting out his truck in this bad weather and go into no store just to call me. I just have to sit here and worry."

"Luke chapter twelve verse twenty-five, 'Can you add a single hour to your life by worrying?'" Jasmine quoted.

"Ohhhh. You're so right, my baby. Thank you so much. I needed that."

Grams' mouth said it, but her actions didn't follow. She chewed on the side of her nails until she was biting her skin. Jasmine had never seen Grams like this. Grams surely never admitted to having any other emotion other than gratefulness to God. Jasmine didn't know how to take this or what to do. She placed her arm around Grams' neck and kissed her.

"Would you feel better if we prayed, Grams?"

"Yes."

"Lord, we thank you for Paw Paw. We ask that you keep him safe out here, especially on days like this. Steady his truck, lighten his loads, clear the roads, straighten his vision, limit his distractions, Oh, God.

"And please ease Grams' mind. Remind her that You are the keeper of Paw Paw, not her. Remind her that You have him in Your arms. Please return him to us in one piece tonight. In Jesus' name. Amen."

"Amen. Thank you so much. You know there's a scripture that says that the unbelieving husband can be saved through the believing wife. I pray for that every day. 'Cause he don't wanna hear nothing about God or Jesus."

"Keep praying for him, Grams. God doesn't sleep, and He doesn't go deaf. Paw Paw is blessed to have a praying woman like you."

"Enough about me. What's with this ten days mess? You can stay here as long as you need."

"I have an apartment that will become available in the next ten days. How did you know that I was pregnant?"

"I heard you throwing up one morning. And you look different in the Spirit realm. The naked eye can't see it. I asked God what was going on with you, and he showed me a baby."

God also showed Grams that the baby wouldn't make it, but Grams knew that Jasmine wasn't ready to hear that. Jasmine wouldn't accept that, so God bridled Grams' tongue and wouldn't allow her to reveal that to her.

Grams continued, "I know this is a new day and time, but I tell you what, back in my day, we started having babies young on purpose. We needed children around to help with the house. I know

147

young ladies these days want to wait until they accomplish this and do that and so on and so forth, but it seems to me that the smarter y'all get, the dumber y'all get.

"For instance, women got so smart that they dumb asses fought for a right to work. Now look at y'all. Tired. Woe out. In college for ten years to work the rest of your life.

"The Bible says that the *man* is to work by the sweat of his brow. But some smart women made it to where women have to work by the sweat of their brows, too.

"Look at my parents and my grandparents. They had all them kids and made it. Never went hungry. Never was homeless. That's just the right order of things if you ask me. The woman stay home and make babies starting young, and the man goes out and works.

"You have me and Wallace. You will be fine. Shoot, when this baby is eighteen, you'll be in your thirties. When your friends' kids are graduating kindergarten, yours will be graduating high school. You'll be just fine."

The door opened. It was Wallace.

"I hate when it rains. Hey, my Honeydew. Hey, Black!"

"Jasmine gonna stay here with us for ten days. She's pregnant, and Shelia put her out."

Wallace stifled his tears. Jasmine had confided the assault to him. He knew this possibly wasn't a baby made by love. He knew that she possibly was in a situation by force.

"My boyfriend got me an apartment. I'll be moving in there in ten days," Jasmine told Wallace.

"Honeydew, let me talk to Jasmine for a second, please."

Grams got up from the table and left.

"Is this pregnancy from what them boys did to you?"

"I don't know because I was also with my boyfriend."

Wallace nodded his head. "You know I'm here for you."

"Yes, Sir."

"We gonna love this baby no matter what."

"Yes, Sir."

"Does John know about what they did to you?"

"No, Sir."

"He's putting you in an apartment. He should. He deserves to know that he may not be the baby's father. And if he can't handle that, you have a place to live here."

"Thank you."

Chapter 29

"John!" his teammate called out to him as he was walking to his car after school.

John turned around. "Wassup, Brice?"

"Say." Brice exhaled, got shifty, fidgety, and began stuttering. "I—I—I don't know all the details of wh-what all went on with you and Damien. Word on the street is—is that he got mad that Jasmine is pregnant. I ain't seen or heard from him since y'all had that fight." Brice exhaled again and slowed his talking down. "It's something you need to know."

Brice reached in his pocket, pulled out a Polaroid picture, and handed it to John. John's face was distorted as he tried to make out the picture. He had to make sure the picture wasn't what he thought it was.

"We all wanted to tell you sooner, but Damien threatened us not to tell, so we didn't. But I can't keep it to myself no longer. They don't know I'm showing you this."

"What the fuck is this?"

"Damien raped Jasmine. You know he's always walking around with that camera. I took the picture."

"Instead of stopping it and helping Jasmine fight him off, you took a picture?!"

"I—I don't know what I was thinking. Man, it was the heat of the moment. And—"

"Are people standing by watching? I see—oh, my God."

John paid closer attention to the picture. While the only clear shot was Damien on top with Jasmine with his hand covering her mouth, in the background he saw three boys with their pants and boxers around their ankles. It was clear that they were watching and waiting on their turns.

"Damien was the ringleader of this. We all just got caught up in the moment. I ain't been able to sleep since this happened months ago."

"Who the fuck is *we*?" John growled.

Brice began stuttering again. He wasn't no snitch. He really just wanted to tell on Damien so that John would handle Damien again, making sure Damien never came back around. He had heard that Damien transferred schools, and he wanted it to stay that way. Brice was afraid of Damien, and he wanted his bully gone for good. He didn't realize that other boys were in the picture naked.

"I'm not finna ask you again," John roared.

"Chris, Tim, Royce—"

"And you."

"And me."

John lunged at Brice and beat the brakes off him. Brice couldn't move fast enough at all. John did it so fast that no one noticed, and there was no attention drawn to them. Once John was finished with Brice, he ran across the parking lot to Tim's car. Tim, Chris, and Royce all rode together every day. Today was no different. Just as Tim was pulling out, John jumped in, pulled Royce out, and began beating him. The others tried to help Royce, but John handled them, too. Now, there was attention.

An officer escorted John to the principal's office. Principal Thomas immediately suspended him from school. John showed the principal a picture of Damien assaulting Jasmine and informed him that the other three guys with their dicks out were Tim, Royce, and Chris. He also told him that Brice was the one who took the picture as he waited on his turn.

Principal Thomas could have flatlined. He couldn't get his thoughts or words together. As he tried to get himself together, he informed John that he would not be suspended, and he apologized for suspending him without knowing the whole story.

"John, I am so sorry for what I am about to tell you. The whole school knows how much you are in love with Jasmine. So much so that it has made its way to my door. I am going to call the cops, but you need to brace yourself for the outcome. I was an officer for thirteen years. I am going to tell you how the law works. You are not going to like what I am about to tell you.

"The only face that is identifiable in this picture is Damien's. The only way Chris, Tim, Royce, and Brice will have to pay for what they did is if they confess to it. You say these penises in the picture belong to Chris, Royce, and Tim. But they are minors. The law is not going to allow officers to ask minors to drop their boxers. Even if the law allowed it, unless there is an identifiable marker on their penises to distinguish them from others, you can't arrest them based on what their penises look like.

"The date on this picture is so long ago that it will not make Jasmine seem credible for pressing charges. Jasmine is not only a Black girl, she is a dark-skinned Black girl. The law is not going to care that a tar child got raped and decided to say something four months later."

John cried into his fists. They weren't tears of sadness, but tears of anger and rage. He couldn't protect Jasmine. The law wasn't going to protect her. Her family didn't protect her. She was unprotected. And for a White man to tell him this, he knew it to be true.

"I'm calling her family now, then I will call the police."

While what Principal Thomas said was true, he didn't have Jasmine's back. He wasn't advocating for her; he was trying to keep drama and attention away from his school. If this made the headlines, oh, my God. People would unenroll themselves from the school, parents would take their money away from the school and out of the school, teachers would quit. It would be a complete shit show.

He also didn't care about her well-being. He viewed her as a sex object like the football players did. A few boys having fun. Not like anyone was really hurt. She wasn't bleeding or anything. She didn't have to go to the hospital or anything like that.

If it was serious, he would have called 911 when he saw it happening that morning during his rounds. He just had no idea that a picture had been taken; he had no idea that proof was lingering. Now, it looked like he couldn't control his students or properly run a school. He couldn't have that.

She had a body that Principal Thomas couldn't stop looking at. She was chubby, so that naturally gave her plump breasts. She was wide hipped and had a big butt. It wasn't the textbook beauty, but it was something about the way she carried it. He wanted a piece of her his damn self. Damn, those football players were lucky.

"Every number that was listed for Jasmine was either disconnected, or someone else had the number. And for whatever reason, she has no address listed. I am outraged! How does Jasmine not have an address listed?!" Principal Thomas said to John.

He never tried to call anyone. He was dialing the wrong numbers on purpose. Her address was staring him right in the face. In addition to that, he knew her Aunt Rosalyn personally from the school conventions he frequently went to. He could have easily called her, but he just didn't care enough to. He didn't care at all.

"It's okay. I know where her parents live. I don't know the address, but I can take the police there. She now lives with her grandparents. I don't know where that is or the phone number there, but I can get you to her parents' house."

Shit! Principal Thomas said underneath his breath.

"Okay. Whew. Good. I'm calling the police now," he told John.

Principal Thomas held on to that picture with his life. He didn't need it getting into the wrong people's hands. When the cops came, they told John the same thing Principal Thomas had told him: they could only go after Damien. They told him that Jasmine was more than welcome to press charges and identify the other boys, but it was so long ago that she wouldn't seem credible.

John was trying to find the silver lining in that Damien could be arrested. The only thing about that was they couldn't find him. The second part was that Jasmine would have to actually say that it was rape and not kinky sex. John couldn't believe what he was hearing.

John took the officers to her parents' house, and they weren't there. No one was there. John got madder. He didn't think that he could.

"John, it's okay. We have the address now. We can come back. We now know where she lives. We will be looking for Damien. If you hear from Jasmine before we do, direct her to the station, Young Man. Okay?"

John nodded his head in agreement.

The officers and John drove away.

Inside Jasmine's parents' house was her dad. He saw the officers and John pull up and assumed they were there to arrest him. Jasmine had been running her mouth about what he had been doing to her, he thought.

I told her to never tell. She's going to pay for this.

Chapter 30

Jasmine was at her grandparents' house completely oblivious to all that had taken place after school on account of her. She was actually having a good day. School was better than it had been since John shut everybody up. The city bus ride to her grandparents' house was smoother than usual. Her grandmother baked a sweet potato pie that tasted like Jesus made it himself. She had no homework to do.

It was a good day.

She asked Grams' permission to call John. She had never called him from their house because she wasn't sure how Grams would take it. But Grams' response shocked her. "You're already pregnant. What else can happen?"

John answered the phone immediately when he saw the name Wallace Jones on his caller i.d. He didn't know who Wallace Jones was, but he hoped it was Jasmine. He knew that her granddad's name was Wallace. "Hello?"

"John!" she answered, excitedly.

"Jasmine." John exhaled. "Hey, Baby."

"This is my grandparents' number."

"Okay."

John had to get the nerve up to tell her all that had happened. Where would he even start?

"We move in together tomorrow! I am so excited!" Jasmine said.

"Me, too, Baby. Mc, too."

There was an awkward silence. That had never happened between them before.

"You okay, John?"

"Baby, I gotta tell you something."

"You can tell me anything. What is it?"

"Um. Brice came to me after school with a picture he took of Damien raping you."

Jasmine's body went limp.

"He told me everything. I think it was everything. He told me that Damien was the ringleader. And that him, Royce, Tim, and Chris followed behind him."

"Oh, my God." Jasmine's voice was trembling.

"And I whupped all they ass in the parking lot. The cops came. I was sent to Principal Thomas's office. I showed him the picture and told him what Brice had told me. He first tried to call your people, but you didn't have a good number with them. The number that is in the phone book is disconnected. He called the cops back, and I took them to your parents' house. Nobody came to the door. They said that they'd keep going by there to tell your parents what happened to you and so that you can press charges.

"They said that pretty much the only one who would have anything happen to them is Damien because he's the one's face we can see on the picture. The rest of them just got their dicks out. And if you press charges on the rest of them, it'd be your word against theirs. Because you waited so long, you won't seem credible."

Jasmine's head was spinning. She heard him, but she didn't hear him. She understood, but she didn't understand. She could barely breathe. She had a sense of relief that it was out there and that John knew, but she was so embarrassed.

There was a picture?! John and the principal saw it?! Who else saw this picture? Who else knew that she had been gang raped? Even though rape is never the victim's fault, that doesn't stop the victim from the feelings of disgust and embarrassment.

"John, I'm sorry I didn't tell you. I was so embarrassed."

"I'm sorry that niggas who call themselves my friends did that to you. I'm sorry that I didn't make you feel safe enough to tell me. I'm sorry that you have gone through this by yourself. I'm so sorry."

"I also don't know if it's yours or the others baby."

"I understand that. You had no control over that. I ain't mad at you. At all. It's okay. I'm still here for you and Journey. We're still moving in tomorrow. Nothing has changed. But you gotta press charges."

"John, I'm not going to. You doing what you did is good enough for me."

"Jas—!"

"John, I've thought a lot about this. And I've prayed a lot about it. I'm not going to be another Black woman helping to destroy a Black man."

"They destroyed themselves! You are a victim!"

"I have never been and will never be that! I am a survivor."

"They need to pay for what they did. They need to wake up every day in a cold cell. They need to fight niggas off from taking they ass every hour. You gonna let them walk free?!"

"They're not free. Now they know that you know, and they know that other people do, too. That's good enough for me."

"I don't agree."

"You don't have to. Just trust me."

Jasmine wasn't sure why something wouldn't let her press charges. She didn't know if it was fear of how they'd retaliate or if she truly believed in letting God get even. But she had peace in knowing that John knew the truth.

She went to the police station with Grams as her support system and told them she wasn't going to press any charges on anybody. The cops didn't care. They didn't try to convince her of anything different. Less work they had to do. On to more important violence and injustices towards White citizens.

Chapter 31

Jasmine and John had been settled into their apartment for about one month. She'd never met his parents. They made it clear that they wanted nothing to do with that bastard baby, whore of a mother, nor stupid ass father who used to be their son. It bothered Jasmine a little, but not enough to stop her from being excited about what was growing inside her. She thought that since she was chubby, she wouldn't show until she was about six months pregnant, but she was wrong. She was a little over four months pregnant, and her stomach was protruding a little. Yes, she was nervous, scared, anxious about being pregnant… but her love for God and Journey overpowered all those feelings.

Grams refused to go to their apartment where they were "shacking and fornicating" as Grams would repeat. Paw Paw went frequently to make sure "that boy treating my grandbaby right." She didn't let her parents or Uncle Daniel and Aunt Rosalyn know where she lived. She gave them her number and ran into them at her grandparents' house, and that was bad enough.

The part she hated was that she didn't see her sisters as often. She saw them on the weekends only when they would all be their grandparents'. Michelle assured Jasmine that Robert had stopped assaulting her, and Jasmine believed her. She always knew when Michelle was lying, and she wasn't.

In addition to being excited about Journey, she was excited about graduation. She was going to be the first doctor in her family. She was sure of that. Getting her high school diploma was the first step.

Her only regret was how she couldn't get E out of her mind. She often thought about the nights they would just ride and vibe out to music. Their "I bet you don't know this song" challenges was what she missed most about him. And oh, my God. He always smelled soooo good.

She told him a month or two ago that she was pregnant and there was no chance it was his. He didn't care that the baby wasn't his. Like John, a baby was taken away from him in utero without his permission. He would love and take care of this baby like his own.

She hadn't talked to him since she told him she was pregnant. She had assured John that there was no chance of E being the dad and that she and E were over. But there was something about today that she couldn't resist him. Hormones? Maybe. Nostalgia being good at her job? Possibly. Whatever the explanation, she broke.

"Hey, E." She was sure to call him from a blocked number. "It's Radio."

"You remember me."

"Don't do that."

"I'm just saying."

"Come get me," she told him.

"Where yo' man at? The one you so in love with and moved in with?"

"He's working until midnight. We got a little time."

"Where I'm getting you from?"

"I'mma catch the bus to the library. And you pick me up in the back. Like old times."

"In Old Times, you were mine."

"I was never yours. You're the one who told me in the beginning that you didn't want a relationship."

"I changed my mind."

"Sorry."

"How long it's gonna take you to get to the library?" he asked her.

"Seventeen minutes."

"I'll be there in thirteen."

They hung up the phone. Jasmine took a quick bath for the *just in case*. She caught the bus to the library, and he was waiting on her as promised.

Damn, he smelled *soooo* good.

After they did what they did that night, she realized that had to be the last time. She couldn't keep doing this. Especially not to John. He was so sweet, kind, understanding, and present. He had put her in an apartment and didn't require her to do anything except be the first doctor in her family. And this is what she did.

"When the next time I'mma see you?" E asked her, as they got dressed in his kitchen.

"We won't. I can't do this to him."

E walked over to Jasmine and kissed her on her cheek. "I understand. The bus stop is at the corner."

"Are you kicking me out?"

"You kicking yourself out. Talking about we won't see each other again. Then get out. Why you here? Bye. I can't drop you off at the library. I can't do that to John," he mocked her.

"If I catch the bus from your house, it'll be an hour, and I have to exchange buses at the bus station. It's dark. I'm not comfortable with that."

"Aww. At least you'll still be home before John gets back from work."

He went to his room and closed the door. Jasmine didn't have time to be emotional about being kicked out his house and being made to ride a city bus she'd never rode and go to the creepy bus station. She had to make it home before John made it home.

****

Jasmine was awakened by John making noise.

"What's going on? What are you doing?" Jasmine asked John.

John continued to put clothes in a duffle bag. "John!"

"Well. Damien is back. He came to my job today. I beat his ass for what he did to you. But that was after he showed me a picture of you getting in the car with E tonight. You know the date be at the bottom of the picture, so I know it was tonight."

He zipped the duffle bag. Jasmine couldn't think of a lie to tell. Even if she could think of a lie, she didn't want to lie. She knew she had to marinate in the consequences of her decisions.

"And I really wanted to believe that there was no way possible he's Journey's dad. But after seeing you be with him tonight, knowing you fucked him with a baby in your belly, I ain't trynna hear that. And if that is my baby, I'm disgusted that you let another man nut on my child. How could you even be comfortable—? You know what? Never mind. Goodnight."

John still sat beside her in class. He didn't want people to know there was trouble in paradise. Not for his sake, but for hers. People were already ugly to her because of her condition. He wasn't going to make it worse.

Jasmine pulled him off to themselves to talk to him at lunch. He wasn't trying to hear anything she had to say. He let her know that he was done with her. He had sacrificed so much, endured so much, lost so much on account of her. He hadn't even talked to his parents in a month on account of her. Possibly lost the opportunity to be a professional football player on account of her.

But he was still good to her. He left her the car so she could drive herself to school while he spent the night at a friend's and caught the city bus. He still carried her books to class and her backpack on his shoulder. He did everything to make it *look like* they were still together, but behind closed doors, he made it clear to her that they were not.

He wanted to move out, but he couldn't find another apartment to approve him because he already had an active apartment in his name. Jasmine was a minor, so no one would approve her.

He told her that she could stay in the apartment. He told her that he'd sleep in Journey's room until Journey came, and he'd sleep on the couch after Journey was born.

She didn't want that. She wanted what they used to have. She wanted to sit up all night and laugh at each other's corny jokes. She wanted to turn over and sleep on his chest. She wanted to bump into him in the mornings as they rushed to get ready to go to school.

She wanted that old thang back. But after living like roommates for 2 weeks, she realized John wasn't coming back.

He never allowed her to explain why she was getting in the car with E. She was kind of relieved because what would she say? What could she say? She couldn't even bring herself to apologize because she was so embarrassed, and an apology would be admitting guilt. She would always flip it and say, "You're mad at what you don't know! If you would just let me explain!" In her mind, that put the ball in John's court to make things right; that took the weight off her.

But she knew she was wrong. And there was no fixing it.

John felt so stupid. Her Aunt Rosalyn tried to warn him about her. His teammates tried to warn him about her. His parents tried to warn him about her. But he wouldn't listen. He so badly wanted that baby that was murdered because of his actions at fourteen that he put all common sense aside. Now, he was paying for it. Literally.

He told her that she had to get a job and they would split the bills down the middle. She didn't like it, but he could have kicked her out and made her go live with her parents again. She loved her grandparents dearly, but she just couldn't live with them. From Grams's overly religious views to Paw Paw's lack of religious views. From Grams singing all the time to Paw Paw fussing all the time. That stuff was fine for the weekends. But day in, day out, it was exhausting. As much as she wanted somewhere free to stay, she wanted somewhere peaceful and conducive for raising a child. Her grandparents' house just wasn't it.

Jasmine began filling out applications, but no one ever called. John saw her trying. He knew it would be hard— her getting a job while pregnant. She was showing beyond reasonable doubt. He knew no one would hire her in that condition. He appreciated her trying. He had mercy on her and never charged her anything. He just requested that she kept the house clean and meals prepared. She made sure she did that.

Chapter 32

"Blackberry! Come help me pick these blackberries off the fence!" Paw Paw called out to Jasmine.

He took it easier on her these days since she was in a family way. But he still loved his talks with her. She wouldn't talk much in the house around Grams and her sisters. So, he would get her alone, keep her busy, and talk to her.

"Paw Paw, I don't want to talk about what you want to talk about," Jasmine said, as they picked the berries. "John handled them all."

"You know, they would make great fertilizer. I really could use more blackberry bushes out here. I'd make a killing."

Jasmine chuckled and rolled her eyes. "You and this dead-body fertilizer."

"I'm just telling you what I heard."

Jasmine shook her head.

She didn't tell him that she and John were over. She was still holding on to hopes that he would come back to her and be with her. She still fantasized about the day that they became more than roommates again.

Until then, she was with E. She knew she shouldn't have been. She knew that lessened the chances of John ever coming back. But she was lonely and desired male companionship. E was willing to give it to her; John wasn't. There was something about E that made her feel so secure and wanted. If John knew that she was still seeing E, he never said anything.

E wasn't a bad guy. He even took her to a doctor's appointment. Journey was healthy and strong. She was right on track with her growth. Yes, Journey was a girl. Jasmine was so excited to have a mini-me. She vowed to protect her always. Journey would never experience any of what she had to experience.

"Journey is a girl, Paw Paw."

Paw Paw stopped picking blackberries and smiled. "I love that. Jasmine, Jr."

"No." Jasmine laughed. "Journey."

"Like traveling?"

"Sure. Like traveling."

She wasn't going to explain the meaning behind the name to him. The only thing Paw Paw understood was working hard and making money. Symbolism and metaphors were way over his head.

They started back picking the blackberries.

"Naming your baby something you ain't never done before? That's like when I see these girls naming their kids Porsche and Mercedes knowing they got knocked up in the back seat of a box Chevy and they driving a broke down Ford. To each its own, though. How John feel about Baby Travel being a girl?"

"He say he gonna be outnumbered in the house. He's still holding on to the faith that she's a boy."

"I been there. Had 2 girls. I still be hoping I'mma find out one is a boy." He bit a blackberry. "Needs better fertilizer."

Jasmine laughed out loud. "Stop it!"

"Hey. I'm just telling you what I heard."

Chapter 33

Jasmine was awakened by a phone call at three in the morning. She immediately answered it for fear of something being wrong with one of her sisters.

"Hello?!" she anxiously answered.

"Jasmine. It's me, your dad."

Her heart dropped into her stomach. Her dad never called her. They hadn't exchanged words since the day she moved out for good. It had to be about Michelle or Denise. Had to be.

"Okay? What's going on?"

"Something been on my mind for a while. I need to talk to you. I know it's late. Or early. However you wanna look at it. But can you come over? Just you."

"I'm on the phone now. Talk."

"It needs to be face to face. Trust me."

She was uneasy about it. Was this just a pawn to get her over there and assault her again? But her nosiness and curiosity wouldn't leave her alone.

She woke John up and told him that she was going over to her parents' house. She gave him their number for the just in case. She never told John about her dad assaulting her. But she did tell him that she was afraid of him.

"I'll go with you," John offered.

"No, thank you. He may not say what he wants to say if you're there."

"He may not do what he wants to do if I'm there, either."

There was a moment of awkward silence.

"I'll be fine," Jasmine finally said.

"I'll drop you off and circle back for you. How about that?"

That made Jasmine feel so much better.

"Yes. Thank you."

When they pulled into the driveway, she saw another vehicle there. That made her feel better to know that someone else was there. That meant he wouldn't try anything.

She walked into the house, and John drove off.

"Jasmine, this is my friend Horace."

Jasmine had never known her dad to have friends. Ever.

"Hi, Mr. Horace."

"Hi, Jasmine."

James began talking. "We need this to go away."

"You need what to go away?" Jasmine asked.

"Your condition," Horace said, as he pointed at her stomach.

"What does my baby have to do with you?"

"My son ain't trynna be no daddy. I ain't trynna be no granddaddy. We got shit to do. Just… fall down some stairs or something."

"What the hell this gotta do with your son? And who *is* your son?"

Damien walked from around the corner. "Me."

Jasmine began feeling lightheaded. Two of her abusers were in the same vicinity as her. Unless John came back soon, it was clear that no one was going to save her.

"My baby has nothing to do with anybody in this room."

"Damien told me that the baby could be his. We don't need you popping up later asking for child support, asking him to take this child to school, needing him to go to PTA meetings. None of that shit. Just do us all a favor and make this go away."

"No," Jasmine replied.

"Listen, you ugly, Black bitch. He paid me real good to make sure this gets handled. We can do this the easy way or the hard way. The ball is in your court."

Jasmine saw a car's headlight shining through the curtains. She silently thanked God that John had come back.

"I'm not getting rid of my baby. Y'all can kiss my ass."

She ran out of the door to get into the car. James ran behind her. He wasn't finished with her.

It wasn't John's car that she saw through the curtains; it was E's. E was the neighborhood's hoodlum. The day before, while James was buying drugs from E, James paid E to get rid of Jasmine. Later that day, E called James and told him that he couldn't do it. He told James that he would give him his money back. James told E that he would

173

just do it himself. He told E the plan just in case E changed his mind.

When E saw James running behind Jasmine, E immediately assumed that James was about to kill her. E took his pistol out and fired it.

Jasmine fell to the ground. She heard the shot, but she didn't feel it. Everything happened so fast that she couldn't process what was going on. It wasn't until she saw her own blood forming a puddle underneath her that she realized that she had indeed been shot.

E got out of his car and ran towards her. He looked to see where she had been shot. He applied pressure to her gunshot wound on the left side of her stomach to slow the bleeding down. He didn't want her to die, just the baby.

Denise saw E shoot Jasmine. The conversation in the living room had woken her up. She didn't know the details of the conversation. She just knew she had heard Jasmine's voice. She was so excited to know that her sister was home that she went into the living room to see her. As she was walking into the living room, Jasmine was running outside, and that's when she saw E shoot Jasmine.

She ran to the kitchen and called 911. For a six-year-old, she was highly intelligent and knew exactly what to say and do once the operator answered the call.

James stopped in his tracks to process what had happened. E told him earlier that he wasn't going to do it, but he did it anyway. James studied E's actions. Either E was a great actor, or he shot Jasmine on accident.

"Don't die, Radio. Don't die," E whispered to her; James couldn't hear what was being said. "You hear me, Radio? Don't die."

James saw that she had been shot in her stomach. He ordered for E to kill her—to shoot her in the head or chest. What was this shot in the stomach about? He told E he would do it himself. Why didn't E let him handle it?

"If she survives this and talks, it is your fault! You were supposed to handle this! The right way!" James whispered to E.

"I couldn't. She's pregnant, Man! And it may be my baby. I told you I couldn't do it! I can't kill the mother of my child," E whispered back.

"You didn't tell me you was fucking her!"

"Wasn't your business! And still ain't!"

"Then why you here if you couldn't do it?"

"To stop you from doing it! You was gone kill her. I got rid of the baby for you. That's really all you wanted anyway."

"I wanted *her* gone. I paid you to get rid of *her*. If I can't have her, nobody can."

E looked at James in disgust."

"I still need all my money back. You didn't do what I paid you to do."

Jasmine was losing blood, and she was losing it quickly. She was hearing James and E talk, but she couldn't focus on it or put it together. Sirens could be heard in the far distance.

"Shit! The cops coming. Hide this gun in your house. We gonna tell them we don't know who did this."

"Bullshit! I ain't putting that weapon in my house and they find it with my fingerprints on it and pin this shit on me."

The sirens were getting closer.

"I swear to God I'll tell Shelia everything if you don't hide this gun."

James ran into the house and hid it in the ottoman without anyone seeing him. He made it back outside before the ambulance and cops showed up. At four am, Jasmine was immediately rushed to the hospital.

James introduced himself to the cops as her dad and E introduced himself to the cops as her friend. James and E both told the cops how she was shot as she was walking out the house. They both played clueless. The cops questioned Horace and Damien; they said the same thing.

By now, Shelia was awake. The police briefed her on what was going on, and she became hysterical. It was her first day off in months; she had slept through it all. No, she and Jasmine didn't get along, but she didn't want her to die. She had even begun looking forward to meeting her grandchild.

The police didn't question Michelle or Robert because it was obvious that they had slept through it all. They didn't question Denise because of her age. The police let everyone go so that they could be with Jasmine during this time. It was unclear if she had life threatening injuries or not. They told the adults to be on standby in case they had more questions or revelations.

As everyone was leaving, John was pulling up. He asked Shelia what was happening, and Shelia told him that Jasmine had been shot and was in the ambulance on the way to the hospital. She told him to follow them. John was sick to his stomach with guilt! *Why did I leave her here by herself?!*

Shelia and the three children rode together. Shelia was a mess. She couldn't get herself together no matter how hard she tried. Michelle was crying. All the memories and thoughts of Jasmine circulated in her head. There was no way she was saying goodbye to her. Robert was emotionless. He just wanted to go back to sleep, and hopefully when he woke up, Jasmine would be dead. Denise was quiet. She had seen the whole thing take place. She's the one who called 911. She didn't know if she had done the right thing or not. She didn't want to get anyone in trouble. She just wanted to save Jasmine's life.

James and E rode together to get their stories straight. They knew that the time would come when the police would separate them and question them separately. They had to make sure both of their stories matched.

James was so upset that E was so sloppy with this. This was not the plan. At all. James had a gun with a silencer on it for when he would kill her himself. He also wouldn't have done it outside for people to see. He was going to do it in the basement. He already had the plastic in place. No noise and no mess. E had messed up everything.

Horace and Damien rode together. Damien asked Horace why they had to go to the hospital. Horace told him, "Because we ain't heartless people. That girl coulda been killed. We don't know. But shit. We can be there for her."

Horace actually had a heart. He didn't want anything bad to happen to Jasmine. He wanted Journey gone, not Jasmine. He just didn't want his son to be a dad.

He didn't know that Damien had raped her. He also didn't know that Damien, E, and James had all come up with a plan together to kill Jasmine. Horace didn't know that this went deeper than a baby.

Damien wanted her dead because his jealousy over her and John had reached a pinnacle, and he didn't know how else to resolve it. John picked her over him. She picked John over him. She didn't want him the way the other girls did. Rejection came at him from every angle with her. He literally couldn't take it.

Because Damien had something to do with E shooting her, Damien didn't want to be anywhere near her. If the police showed up at the hospital, Damien didn't want to be there to be questioned again. He wanted to wash his hands of this.

Jasmine was in surgery when they arrived. Robert, Denise, Michelle, James, Shelia, Rosalyn, Daniel, Wallace, Darlene, Horace, E, John, and Damien all waited around for the verdict. There were silent stares between Horace, Damien, James, and E that said, *You better not say shit! Don't break!*

The doctor entered the lobby and asked to speak to Shelia. Shelia's knees bumped as she walked towards him.

"She's well," Doctor Thornton began. "She's going to make a full recovery. She will be back walking and doing everything she did before. No life threatening or life altering injuries... to her. But we could not save the baby."

Shelia got a lump in her throat, trying to hold back tears. She had lost a baby before. She wouldn't wish that pain on anyone. Not even on her daughter who she hated.

"We've allowed her some time with her baby girl. She's still with her daughter. Because she was six months pregnant, the baby was a body. There will have to be a burial for the baby. A death certificate will be issued. Jasmine is very emotional right now. Once the pain meds wear off, she'll be able to feel emotions way more, and she'll really be emotional. Please be sensitive to her needs. She's in room forty-two. You may go in whenever you're ready."

Shelia wiped her tears, took a deep breath, and told everyone what the doctor said. The happiness inside of Rosalyn couldn't be measured. Even though Jasmine had said the baby couldn't be Daniel's, Rosalyn couldn't be too sure. Now that there was no baby, it didn't matter. Daniel wouldn't have a child roaming this earth that didn't come from his wife. Now she could have her husband all to herself again.

Horace thought he would be happy to hear that. But now that he was hearing it, he wasn't. A baby would have to be buried. He couldn't celebrate that. A life was taken. That was nothing to rejoice over.

Damien was happy that the baby was gone, but he wanted Jasmine gone, too. He thought about finishing the job himself.

E was sick. He did this. The pain, sorrow, depression that she was feeling was because of him. *Why didn't I just shoot her in the leg? The hand? Anywhere but her stomach? Did she see me do it?*

James, like Damien, was pissed that Jasmine still had breath in her body. And he wondered how much of his and E's conversation did she hear and/or remember.

Daniel was indifferent. He just wanted to go to work. He was missing money behind this bitter blackberry.

Wallace knew that Jasmine loved her baby because she named her. Jasmine talked about Journey as if Journey was already home in a bassinet. How could he comfort his sweet blackberry?

Darlene sung to herself and prayed. That baby was conceived out of wedlock. That baby was not God's plan. This was bound to happen one way or another.

Shelia walked into Jasmine's room and saw Jasmine rocking and singing to her deceased daughter. Shelia remembered doing the same thing to her child that she miscarried. Jasmine looked up at Shelia and continued singing to Journey Rose Hines.

Shelia sat down on the bed and allowed Jasmine and Journey to have their time. She said nothing to Jasmine, and Jasmine said nothing to her. After sitting in silence for forty-five minutes, Shelia left the room. She would allow someone else the opportunity to spend time with Jasmine and Journey.

When she went back to the lobby, she saw Damien, James, and E being escorted out in handcuffs. She went berserk. "Let my husband go! He did nothing! Let him go!"

An officer restrained her and let her know what had happened. The officers had gone to the hospital to question Denise because she was the one who called 911. Denise told them that E shot her. Denise also told the officers that she had overheard James, Damien, and E in the basement discussing killing her before James handed E money.

When the cops questioned E, he realized that if they were to test him, he had gun powder residue on him. He was so caught up in all that had gone on

that he didn't wash his hands. He never had the time
to bathe or change clothes. He would be found
guilty anyway, so there was no need in lying. He
figured if he cooperated, they would take it easier
on him.

When James made the statement to him, "If I
can't have her, no one can," E knew that Jasmine
was James's sexual victim. James never expounded
to E why he wanted her killed. He paid E money to
handle a job; a book of explanations wasn't needed.
E knew not to ask why because that's the rule in the
game. But he wondered why James would want his
daughter killed.

All E knew was that he couldn't let Jasmine be
killed, so he interfered and botched James's plan.
He snitched on James so that Jasmine could be free
of him. He snitched on Damien so that she could be
free of someone who wanted her dead.

Wallace watched all of this unfold. He was
angry that the cops got to them before he did. He
wanted to handle it himself. He really wanted to
make fertilizer out of anyone who hurt his
Blackberry, but it was now out of his control. The
only thing for him left to do was to focus on
Jasmine. He walked into her room to check on her.
He saw her with Journey, and his heart cracked.

"Can I hold her?" he asked Jasmine.

It snapped Jasmine out of the daze she was in.
"Sure."

She handed Journey to her Paw Paw. He wasn't
prepared for how the baby looked. Journey was

gray, swollen, and just downright scary looking.
She looked like she was straight out of a horror
movie. But he spent time with her anyway. That
was his first great grandchild. He would love her
forever.

"Put her in the bassinet once you're done. I've
had all the time I want with her. I'm fine now."

He knew that was the drugs talking. She would
never be fine.

"Black, do you remember what happened?"

"Yeah. I remember everything."

He looked at her, hoping she would talk.

"I remember everything," she repeated.

"E, James, and Damien got arrested for this."

"Why Damien?"

"All three of them worked together to kill you.
But from what I got from the story, E didn't want to
kill you, but he had to shoot you to stop James from
killing you. If E wouldn't have shot you, James was
going to kill you."

Jasmine slowly nodded her head. She
remembered hearing that when E and James were
talking. She knew that Damien hated her, but she
didn't know it was to the point of wanting her dead.
She didn't even press charges against him for raping
her when the proof was right there on the picture,
and he still did that to her?!

The medications that were in her system had
her filters off. Her mouth ran like a faucet to Paw
Paw. She told him everything. From James to
Daniel to the football players' names. From her

mom doing nothing about it to Rosalyn accusing her of trying to take her man from her. Jasmine told it all. She even told him about the possibility of Rosalyn trying to kill her.

She didn't tell him about Michelle and Robert. She wasn't that loopy. She remembered her promise to Michelle. Michelle said that Robert had stopped, so there was no need to tell him.

"Everything is going to be okay, Black. They won't hurt you again. You have my word. I know about this now. None of this will happen again. If the justice system fumble the ball, I'mma pick it up. Okay?"

Jasmine nodded her head. She wasn't worried. They had been arrested, Uncle Daniel hadn't touched her in months, and John had handled the football players. There was nothing left for Paw Paw to do. Everything had been handled.

Michelle and Denise came into her room. Michelle told Jasmine that Denise was the one who saw everything and called 911. Jasmine told Denise that she was so proud of her and that she did the right thing. She also apologized to Denise for having to see and hear all of that.

Denise had a lot of questions about "this dead baby laying here". Jasmine understood that she was only six and was going to have questions, but she just wasn't in the mood for them. She was trying to understand everything and deal with it herself. She didn't have the energy to explain things just yet.

"Sister is tired, Denise. Let's let her go to sleep," Michelle told her.

"Okay. Hurry up and get better so we can pick blackberries off the fence, Jasmine. I have to tell you about Aladdin."

"Okay." Jasmine smiled and chuckled.

John came in once Michelle and Denise left. Jasmine sobbed on his chest. All the emotions she had been hiding landed on his shirt. She didn't have to be anyone but herself around John, and she was so grateful for his presence.

She was so apologetic, and he was so forgiving. He apologized to her for leaving her at her parents' house by herself. She didn't blame him at all. She was just grateful that he was there.

John picked up Journey. "She has my nose," he said, with tears in his eyes.

And she did.

Jasmine allowed him to have all the time he wanted with her. She knew he thought about his aborted friend's child every second. Now, he would think about Journey every second as well.

"The nurse said that you can do a DNA test if we want to. Can you do it for me? I wanna know," Jasmine said.

"Okay."

"I'll let you know the results when they come in."

John thought about it. "Nah. She looks just like me. I already know."

Chapter 34

Jasmine returned to school despite everyone telling her not to. She was all over the news. Paw Paw, Grams, and John felt like she didn't need that attention. They had already been whispering about her and loudly being ugly towards her before the shooting and miscarriage. This was going to be worse.

But when she was pregnant, she vowed to not let emotions make her hide. She meant that. Even though the principal was going to let her finish school at home, Jasmine still went to school every day. She said that if she allowed emotions to run her out of high school, she would allow emotions to run her out of college, job opportunities, life. She wasn't going to start that habit. She was going to be like David in the Bible and face this Goliath head on.

One month after the shooting, she graduated high school. She was going to be the first doctor in her family. She made that promise to herself and Journey.

While her classmates were celebrating graduation by sneaking into clubs, having house parties, driving out of town, and causing chaos in establishments, she spent her night at Journey's grave.

"I brought the juice," she said to the tombstone, "and my fancy hat." She made her graduation cap do a little dance. "Your mother will be a doctor one day. I promise."

Jasmine reached into her pocket and unfolded a piece of paper. "Got this in the mail the other day. I know you can't read, yet, so I'll read it to you. John is your dad."

Jasmine was happy that he was, but she hated that he was. That meant that he lost two children. She hated that she caused him that pain again. She wouldn't tell him he was the biological father because, like he said, he already knew. But if he ever asked, she would tell him.

John and Jasmine were not giving their relationship another try just yet. John said he didn't know if he wanted her back. He forgave, but he didn't forget.

They were still living together and both vowed that they were going to focus on their careers. A college football team had picked up John, and he was going to see where that took him.

"Well, on Monday, E, James, and Damien will have a hearing for bail. They all pled guilty in hopes it'll get them lesser time. I pray they all get denied bail. They put you here in this grave. They never need to see the light of day again."

Chapter 35

"How the hell James, E, and Damien get out on bond when they admitted to the shit?!" Paw Paw Wallace roared, as his palms hit the wooden kitchen table over and over again.

"It's because no one cares about a Black girl being abused. If Jasmine was a White girl with blue eyes and blonde hair, they would never see the light of day again," Grams answered.

"Naw. If she was a light skinned mulatto with pretty hair, they would never see the light of day again. But because she can't pass a paper bag test and can camouflage with a blackberry, who the fuck cares? Because water sits on top of her hair instead of flowing through it, these niggas can walk free. I tell you what. They fucked with the right Black nappy headed girl this time!"

"Wallace," Darlene pleaded. "You know your pressure been up. You have to calm down."

"Calm down? Calm down?! After what they did?! After what James been doing to our Blackberry for years?! I tell you what. You calm down while I turn this whole fucking state red!"

Wallace grabbed his keys and didn't return home until the next day. When he walked through the door the next day, he immediately took his clothes off to take a shower. He had to wash yesterday off of him.

"Wallace," Darlene called his name, as she peeped around the corner at him.

"Hey, Sweet Pea. I'm sorry about yesterday. Black is just my baby. And they ruined her. They ruined my baby, Darlene." Tears flooded his face.

"I know. But we have to trust that the justice system and Jesus will work in our favor."

"Darlene. The justice system nor Jesus was designed for Blacks. You trust them and pray while I load the shotgun."

"No, Wallace."

"Darlene, I did twelve years in the pen because I trusted the 'justice system', and our sweet Black China Doll is damaged goods because Jesus sat His ass up there and did what He do best: not a damn thang! I don't wanna hear shit else about your White justice system or your White Jesus!"

Darlene stood there, going back and forth in her mind, battling whether to fight with him or allow him to feel what he had a right to feel. She decided on the latter.

"Darlene. I'm sorry." He hugged her, and she hugged him back. He reached into his pocket and gave her some money. "Get away from all this and me for a few days. Go visit your sisters in Shreveport. That's enough for gas money and for y'all to go to the theater and watch *Sister Act 2*. Go. Enjoy yourself."

"Really?"

"Yes. I know your sisters always make you feel better. You need to go through this with them.

We'll be okay down here. If anything comes up, you're just four hours away. You can make it back in good timing. Go. Enjoy yourself. I'll hold down the fort."

"Thank you so much, Wallace. I can't wait to call my sisters and tell them I'm coming!"

"I can't wait, either. Y'all tying up my phone line all damn day."

"If you would just pay for call waiting—"

"Pray that Jesus will give me enough money to pay for it," he sarcastically said.

Darlene playfully hit his chest, kissed him, packed her bags, and left for Shreveport, Louisiana to see her three sisters. Wallace was relieved. There was a chance that she wouldn't accept the offer to leave. He was so glad that she did. He needed to get rid of her to do what he needed to do. He really, really needed to wash yesterday off of him.

Chapter 36

Darlene spent five days with her sisters.
Wallace didn't rush her to come back home. He told
her to take all the time she needed. But judging the
way he sounded over the phone, she needed to go
home. She had known him since she was twelve
years old. She was now sixty. She knew when her
husband's mind was slipping. Something wasn't
right with him.

When she arrived home, he was in the backyard
planting more blackberry trees, blackberry bushes,
and tomatoes. He had gone manic. He was bipolar,
and he kept it under wraps pretty well. But she
knew that this would be the thing that would push
him over the edge.

"Hey, Sweetie," Darlene spoke to him, careful
not to alert him.

He looked up from gardening. "Hey, Sweet
Pea. Why you back so early?"

"I needed to check on you."

"I'm fine. Go back."

"What you been doing?" she asked him.

"Planting. Gardening. Plucking. Toiling the
ground. Growing me more blackberries like I been
talking about doing for years. Finally finna grow
them tomatoes. Maybe even start me a corn maze.
Shit. Some potatoes, too, if they all get along back
here and got room. I'mma make us some money.
I'm selling everything I grow."

He was moving and speaking so fast. He was in a full blown manic stage.

"Okay. That's good."

"Just occupying my time. You know what they did to my sweet Blackberry. And they let them out on bail. And probably gonna let them off real easy. You know how they feel about a dark-skinned girl. Black didn't deserve this. None of it."

"I talked to Jasmine. She's taking it pretty well," Grams said.

"Jasmine takes everything pretty well. But I ain't Jasmine, and Jasmine ain't me."

"Wallace."

"Get from back here, Darlene. You got Jesus. I got gardening. I don't bother you while you pray. Don't bother me while I plant. Gone on now. Get!"

Darlene went in the house. "*Fix it , Jesus. You know all about it, God. Solve the problem, Jesus. Only you can,*" she sang.

All day and all night, he was out there. She didn't understand much about gardening. She didn't know if it took that long or not. But there were plenty days where she prayed all day and night. Like he said, him planting was him praying. If it took him all night, then she would leave him at it. He was safe and well back there. That's all that mattered.

Chapter 37

"Hello?" Wallace answered the phone.

"Daddy. Have you seen or heard from Daniel?" Rosalyn asked him.

"What?!"

"I haven't heard from him in a week. I was trying to keep it to myself, but, Daddy. This is my husband. I have spent many years with him. I love him. He is my lifeline. Do you have any idea where he is?"

"Rosalyn, I know you're not asking me to care about a man who harmed my Black China Doll. I'mma give you another chance to clear up why you're calling me."

Rosalyn was silent.

"And you knew what your sick ass husband was doing to your niece. You can't tell me you didn't know. But you been jealous of Shelia ever since she had Jasmine because you can't have kids. And you can't have kids because that sick bastard ex-boyfriend of yours raped you in college, gave you a disease, and that disease made you not able to ever have children. So you've hated Jasmine her whole life because she was the reminder of what you'll never be—a mama.

"But for you to sit back and do nothing about your husband raping your *blood* makes you sicker than him. I don't know where that motherfucker at. I don't care. I pray to whatever God exists that the

Ku Klux Klan has gotten ahold of him, set him on fire, and right before he kissed death, they resuscitated him, and kept him just enough alive so that he will suffer.

"And I pray that once he gets back well, they'll do the shit again. And I pray they find you and do the same thing to you."

Wallace hung up the phone.

Darlene usually kept him levelheaded in times like this. But this was beyond her. There was nothing that she could do. Shit had hit the fan, and it was spinning. It was a nonstop chaotic riot in Wallace's mind. He turned on the TV to let his mind drift away, but that backfired.

"…James Hines, who is facing charges for raping and conspiring to kill his daughter, failed to show up to court today. When a wellness check was done on him, he was not home or reachable. No one knows his whereabouts…

"Damien Brumfield was also supposed to show up in court today for sentencing for conspiracy to murder the same young lady. When he failed to show up to court, a wellness check was done on him as well. No one knows his whereabouts, either…"

Darlene looked at Wallace and Wallace looked at Darlene. Darlene gulped.

"They shouldn't have ever let them out. They gonna get away with it. I told you. I told you! And they ain't gonna look for them. The justice system don't give a damn about Jasmine. Ain't shit gonna be done!"

The phone rang. Wallace ran to answer it. "Hello?!"

"Just tell me it's going to be okay, Paw Paw. Just tell me that."

Wallace exhaled. "Blackberry, don't you worry your pretty little head. I gave you my word that everything will be okay. I told you that if the justice system fumbled the ball, I would pick it up. When have you known me to lie to you?"

"I know," she whined, "but they're missing. That means they're free. Free to finish the job."

"No! No! That ain't gonna happen!"

"You don't know that, Paw Paw!"

"Yes, I do! I ain't never lied to you. I ain't gonna start now. You let me take care of this. I'll worry about this for the both of us. I got this."

He hung up the phone and massaged his temple.

"Wallace, take your meds to calm you down. I'm afraid you're gonna become too amped up."

Wallace pretended to take his meds, but he didn't. He spit them out as soon as she turned her back. He needed the amp. He needed to halfway be out of his mind. He wanted to feel everything that this situation brought. He didn't want anything to numb the pain.

He went to the backyard and got to gardening. All of his energy, frustration, worries, and agitations went into his garden.

"Do you know where James is at, Shelia? And don't you lie to me. I'm your mother." Grams said to Shelia over the phone.

"No, I do not. But the same day Rosalyn said Daniel went missing is the same day James went missing. So, they're somewhere living it up. I'm pretty sure they in another state, praying no one notices them. And I bet they got Damien with them. The three of them gonna make a new life for themselves."

Shelia sniffed her tears away.

"I don't know how I'mma make it without his income. He stopped getting checks once he was arrested. At least he was selling drugs to get us through. But now that he's gone, that money is gone, too. My whole life is upside down. I can't even catch my breath. Why is this happening to me?!"

"How do you think Jasmine feels? Her little world?" Darlene asked Shelia.

"Jasmine is young. She can bounce back and adjust. She's in college. She's going to be a doctor one day. She is just fine. It's me. I'm the one suffering! I have three kids in this house to take care of. She's living the good life with John. Jasmine is living good. I'm the victim!"

Darlene felt herself emotionally going to a place that Jesus couldn't rescue her from. She hung up in Shelia's face before she told her something that would cause her to repent later.

"Serving the Lord will pay off after while. Serving God will pay off after while. Oh yeah. Just keep working every day. Whatever is right, God said He would pay. Serving the Lord, I know, it will pay off after while. I got to keep on working. Yes, I have. 'Cause I want my starry crown. I know that my way will get righter even though my friends sometimes let me down. And oh, what a time it will be when my Savior, my Savior face I see. Serving the Lord—it'll pay off after while," Darlene sang to herself, as she watched Wallace in the back yard.

She then reevaluated her way of thinking and her beliefs as it came down to little girls and their bodies and their rights. She became angry at what she once thought was right and acceptable.

She now understood why Wallace was in the backyard gardening so much. She grabbed a shovel and helped him. He looked at her; she looked at him. They said nothing to each other and spoke nothing of it. He manipulated the ground, and she rearranged the dirt.

"What a friend we have in Jesus. All our sins and griefs to bear. What a privilege to carry everything to God in prayer…," Grams sang, as she and Paw Paw dug away the problems.

Chapter 38

"James, Damien, and Daniel been missing for about eight months now. Guess they're hiding from the cops. And Wallace wanna get a hold to them so bad that he can't do nothing but drive them trucks and work in that damn yard on them blackberries. He done planted blackberry bushes, blackberry trees, blackberry fields, blackberry blackberries! At least it's paying off. People knocking on our door all day and night to buy them blackberries. Only God knows how he's growing 'em so fast. Whatever he's doing, it's keeping his mind half-way sane. I hope the police get a hold of James, Damien, and Daniel before Wallace do. Whatever Wallace do to them, ain't no coming back from," Darlene told her sister Rita.

"You think Wallace feels guilty?" Rita asked. "Guilty that he didn't know what was going on with Jasmine?"

"Oh, yes. He feels guilty that he didn't trust his gut when his gut told him that James and Daniel were messing with her. He feels guilty that he didn't do anything then and that he can't do anything now."

"I talk to Jasmine a lot. She's been doing good. Got herself straight A's," Rita said.

"Jasmine is going to always have straight As. Girl couldn't fail if she tried."

Two semesters had passed since they went missing. Jasmine buried herself so deep into her schoolwork to get her mind off of things that she had no choice but to get straight As. She lived in fear every second that they were coming back to kill her.

She was always paranoid that they were somewhere lingering around. *Are they watching me from the back of the class? Are they watching me at work from across the street? Are they in the parking lot waiting on me to get out of church? The lights just went out. Was that the storm, or was that them?*

Paranoia flooded her brain and emotions constantly. At least E was serving his time peacefully and gracefully. But E was never her concern.

John hated himself every second for not killing Damien when he had the chance. That night when Damien popped up at John's job with a picture of Jasmine getting in the car with E, he had thoughts of beating his head in with a crowbar, but he didn't. When he asked Damien why he raped Jasmine, Damien answered him, "I did it to protect you." That made absolutely no sense. "You raped, abused, humiliated my girl to protect me? How? How did doing that protect me?!"

John never gave him a chance to answer. John beat his ass right then and there. Seeing on the news that Damien was missing made John regret stopping beating his ass. He was also mad at Jasmine for not pressing charges on him when she had the chance.

He wouldn't have had the opportunity to conspire to murder her if he was already locked up. Even if he conspired from behind bars, he wouldn't have had the opportunity to flee on bail. Maybe he still would have. Who knows? John just knew that he was angry.

He lost his baby to Damien. Jasmine was a ball of emotions because of Damien. Every time he reached to touch her, she pulled back because of Damien. She could never relax. He hadn't seen her smile in so long. He couldn't remember what her laugh even sounded like.

Damien needed to be found. And when he was found, he needed to die.

Chapter 39

"Blackberry, let's pick some berries off the fence," Wallace said to Jasmine.

Jasmine didn't mind picking the blackberries anymore. Her hands and wrists were no longer sore. And she loved the talks with Wallace. Whether they made sense or not, he was a delight to be around.

"Tell me. How are you really?" he asked her.

"I am relieved and nervous."

"How so?"

"Relieved that Daddy is not hurting me anymore. Relieved that I am free from the hell he had me living in. I am relieved that I am no longer pregnant. Even though I loved my baby and had so many plans for her and with her, I wasn't ready. I have nothing to give a child right now. I'm still a child in so many ways.

"I am nervous because I am so scared that Daddy is going to pop back up, and the abuse will start again. I'll be honest, Paw Paw. I do not care that he is missing. I hope he stays gone. I don't mean to pray that he terrorizes somebody else. I just pray that if he still wants to terrorize somebody, he doesn't choose me. The same for Uncle Daniel. The same for Damien."

Wallace stopped Jasmine from picking the blackberries, grabbed her shoulders, looked her in her eyes, and talked. "I ain't no religious man. But when I saw you walk into my house after the accident, my heart thanked God. You didn't roll in my house in a wheelchair. You have all your limbs. You ain't in a cemetery. You are alive and well.

"And you have the rest of your life to be a mama. I'm sorry you lost Journey. Journey will forever be a part of you. We can even throw a get-together of some kind or a birthday party every year on her birthday if you want to. You don't ever have to forget Journey. I don't ever want to forget Journey. Journey was my great grandbaby, and I know Journey woulda been as chocolate and greedy as you. I woulda had to drive three trucks at a time to keep up with y'all bellies.

"I don't want you to think that you and John the only ones who love Baby Travel. I love her, too. I think about her all the time. I ain't never held a dead baby before, but I had to hold her. I had to spend a few seconds with her. I had started planning with her in my head, too.

"Our weekends were gonna be on and poppin'! You was gone hate me. I was gone feed her candy for breakfast, cookies for lunch, and cake for dinner. Then I'd send her home to you.

"I was gonna tell her all the stories about my parents. She was gonna have the newest pair of grocery store tennis shoes. I was gone comb her hair and put in bows bigger than her head.

"She was gonna be my riding partner in my trucks until she was old enough to go to school. I was gonna teach her how to drive as soon as her feet reached the pedal. I was gonna teach her how to double dutch."

Wallace wiped the few tears that managed to find their way down his cheeks.

"I was gonna be right here for you, Black. Here for you and John. Y'all some good kids. I wasn't gonna turn my back on you. I'm still not. Whatever y'all need, I'm here. Y'all really are some good kids out here trying to do the right thing. I can't do nothing but respect that.

"And as far as James, Damien, and Daniel coming back. Well. You know my side business of selling them blackberries really booming. Can't retire from the trucks, but it's paying some bills. Darlene traveling back and forth to Shreveport to visit her sisters more than she used to. We can afford the gas for her to run the streets, thanks to them blackberries. At this rate, gas gonna be one dollar a gallon! Ain't no way gas can get higher than that.

"But them blackberries selling so good that it's keeping gas in both of our vehicles. Turns out dead bodies do make whatever you're growing grow faster. I told you I heard that dead bodies make great fertilizer. I got James, Daniel, Damien, and those four football players to thank for all these blackberries on the fence."

BOOKCLUB DISCUSSION QUESTIONS

1. Do you think John was a pedophile who should serve time for getting Jasmine pregnant when he was eighteen (an adult), and Jasmine was seventeen (a minor)?
2. Do you think Grams knew that Wallace had buried those bodies in the backyard?
3. Should Jasmine have told Paw Paw about Robert assaulting Michelle?
4. Did Robert get off the hook too easily as it pertained to the assault he caused on Michelle?
5. Was Shelia aware of Michelle being assaulted and ignored it like she did with Jasmine being assaulted?
6. Was John not suspicious enough about the things that were going on at home with Jasmine with John and Daniel?
7. Did E really prove his loyalty to Jasmine, or was this betrayal?
8. Should Paw Paw have handled Jasmine's abusers differently? Should he have allowed the justice system to punish them instead?
9. If Jasmine would have given her mom proof that her dad was abusing her, leaving no room for doubt, what do you think Shelia would have done about James?
10. Who was the biggest villain in the story?

THANK YOUS

Thank you, God for allowing the message to outshine the traumas. Thank you for the ability to triumph through everyday battles so that a milestone could be achieved, and for discrimination, in any form, to be laid to rest. Thank you for the village and the tribe you've set forth so that every little Black girl knows there is hope and comfort in tomorrow. God, thank you for giving me the inspiration to travel this journey and be a vessel to others. Thank you.

Mama, you set a standard for me to always keep God first and never settle for less. Your support and love for my success have always been unmatched.

Granny, thank you for showing me that little Black girls win, too. Your constant, guiding light and prayers paved a way for me, even in the midst of my storms.

A special thank you to LaJerika and Ellise for the constant motivation, encouragement, and assurance as I continue along this path.

Thank you to all my sisters who have supported me throughout this journey.

I LOVE EACH ONE OF YOU DEARLY.

To my amazing, God-fearing, wonderful, and blessed editor, you, my dear, are among the few women who I wholeheartedly trust. When the time came to begin writing this book, I asked God to seal my concerns into someone who could truly help execute my vision and thoughts onto paper. You have done just that. We were bound as girls in the classroom; now, we're "bound" as grown, successful Black women making a way for the upcoming generation. I truly thank you from the bottom of my heart. I couldn't do this without you!

Last, but certainly not least, I have to pat myself on the back. No one truly knows how dark the road gets, especially when you're traveling it alone and depending solely on God for help and strength. The unanswered questions, the uncertainties, the feelings of being overlooked and inadequate—those days are over. Here's to that little, dark skinned, tomboyish, slightly chubby, outspoken, intelligent, beautiful Black girl. I LOVE YOU. I AM YOU.

Thank you for reading! Please leave a review wherever reviews are accepted!

www.ingramcontent.com/pod-product-compliance
Lightning Source LLC
Chambersburg PA
CBHW050343030726
47503CB00008B/2586